She was sleeping with the lights on.

Kevin sat in the darkness of his upstairs bedroom, watching Beth's house, waiting for someone to attempt another attack.

What had that been about earlier? Bantering clever words? Making promises? Touching her?

If he hadn't realized long ago how stupid it was for him to care about someone, would he have tugged on Beth's hand and pulled her into his arms? He'd wanted to. She wasn't part of the plan he'd made for his life, wasn't a case he'd been assigned to, wasn't someone he should be worried about even now—yet every male cell in him had wanted to wrap his body around hers and chase the fear from those muted blue eyes.

Traitorous hormones weren't the only thing keeping him awake, however.

There was something about that whole crime scene that nagged him—something he couldn't yet put his finger on.

Kevin had written off pretty women who showed any interest in him. Yet here he was, keeping a lonely vigil over Beth Rogers.

Logic and experience told him to assign watchdog duty to someone else. It was the curse of his conscience—and his need to protect this innocent beauty—that prevented him.

JULIE MILLER

BEAUTY *and the* BADGE

HARLEQUIN®

TORONTO • NEW YORK • LONDON
AMSTERDAM • PARIS • SYDNEY • HAMBURG
STOCKHOLM • ATHENS • TOKYO • MILAN • MADRID
PRAGUE • WARSAW • BUDAPEST • AUCKLAND

For my good friends Eric and Jeri and sweet little Ella.
It's like having family here in Nebraska.

And for Connie, of course. Because she's such a big fan.

Recycling programs
for this product may
not exist in your area.

ISBN-13: 978-0-373-88950-1

BEAUTY AND THE BADGE

Copyright © 2009 by Julie Miller

www.eHarlequin.com

Printed in U.S.A.

ABOUT THE AUTHOR

Julie Miller attributes her passion for writing romance to all those fairy tales she read growing up, and to shyness. Encouragement from her family to write down all those feelings she couldn't express became a love for the written word. She gets continued support from her fellow members of the Prairieland Romance Writers, where she serves as the resident "grammar goddess." This award-winning author and teacher has published several paranormal romances. Inspired by the likes of Agatha Christie and Encyclopedia Brown, Ms. Miller believes the only thing better than a good mystery is a good romance.

Born and raised in Missouri, she now lives in Nebraska with her husband, son and smiling guard dog, Maxie. Write to Julie at P.O. Box 5162, Grand Island, NE 68802-5162.

Books by Julie Miller

HARLEQUIN INTRIGUE

841—POLICE BUSINESS*
880—FORBIDDEN CAPTOR
898—SEARCH AND SEIZURE*
947—BABY JANE DOE*
966—BEAST IN THE TOWER
1009—UP AGAINST THE WALL**
1015—NINE-MONTH PROTECTOR**
1070—PROTECTIVE INSTINCTS†
1073—ARMED AND DEVASTATING†
1090—PRIVATE S.W.A.T TAKEOVER†
1099—KANSAS CITY CHRISTMAS†
1138—PULLING THE TRIGGER
1176—BEAUTY AND THE BADGE†

*The Precinct
**The Precinct: Vice Squad
†The Precinct: Brotherhood of the Badge

CAST OF CHARACTERS

Detective Kevin Grove, KCPD—When his beautiful new neighbor—bloodied and frightened by an attack at her home—wakes him in the middle of a cold, wintry night, this "beast" of a man reluctantly steps into the role of her protector.

Elisabeth (Beth) Rogers—Small-town girl in the big city—just doing her job and making a life for herself. Who'd want to terrorize her?

Miriam Grove—Kevin's grandmother. Her body may be failing her, but her mind is still razor sharp.

Charles Landon—VP of research and development and Beth's boss at GlennCo Pharmaceuticals. He sees a lot of potential in his young executive assistant.

Deborah Landon—Charles's fourth wife never misses a morning rendezvous.

Raymond Glenn—CEO of GlennCo Pharmaceuticals.

Geneva Landon—Charles's first wife. She's VP of public relations and a board member at GlennCo.

Tyler James—Chief of the GlennCo security team. He has a hands-on approach to keeping company employees—and secrets—safe.

Atticus Kincaid—Kevin's partner at KCPD.

Daisy—Part mastiff, part pit bull, part couch potato.

Chapter One

"Yes, Mom. I'll do everything I can to get home for Christmas. Oops."

Too fast.

What a surprise.

Elisabeth Rogers hunched her shoulder to catch her cell phone between her ear and the thick wool scarf she wore, and grabbed the steering wheel with both hands to make the turn onto the snow-packed streets of her neighborhood. Her midsize Jeep swung around the corner and slid into an icy rut in the opposite lane, spinning for a moment before the tires found traction and shot forward.

No accident. No problem. Exhaling a foggy breath of relief as she slowed her speed and moved to the right side of the street, Beth peered through her windshield into the frozen night, promising to buy herself a hands-free phone so she could negotiate the Kansas City streets more safely.

She'd been driving this route home by herself every night for the past four months. She'd driven wintry farm roads back in central Missouri since she was fifteen. She knew better than to be in such a rush.

It was just all that weirdness at work today that left her a little unsettled and anxious to kick off her boots and put up her feet in the quiet security of her own space. Her boss, Charles Landon, the vice president of Research and Development at GlennCo Pharmaceuticals, had sent her to lunch and then disappeared for the rest of the day without an explanation or even leaving his phone on, forcing her to take one meeting for him and reschedule another. Not that she minded thinking on her feet or running the office—Elisabeth was ready and eager to do more than work as an executive assistant. But, at twenty-five, she knew she still had a lot to learn about the world of big business— she had connections to make, opportunities to develop, dues to pay.

When he'd come back as she was on her

way out the door at 5:30 p.m., turned on his fatherly charm and begged her to stay, she'd agreed to work late. It was part of those dues to stay until 9:00 p.m. to type in updates for meeting presentations, revise his schedule—and consequently, her own—and place a couple of overseas phone calls to verify end-of-the-year accountability reports. Despite his apology and claim that he'd been taking care of some personal business that was nothing for her to worry about, she'd sensed an agitation beneath Charles's affable persona that concerned her.

He'd seemed distracted, unable to focus. When he didn't respond to her announcement that she was leaving, she'd gone into his office and found him crawling under his desk to retrieve a pen he'd dropped. He'd snapped at her offer to help him look, then smoothed his gray hair back and apologized as he pulled his pen from the pocket of his pinstriped suit.

"Weird," Beth mouthed. "Totally weird night." She fished her phone from the folds of her scarf and tucked it back up against her ear. "Mom? You still there?"

"Why didn't you wait until you got home

to call?" Ellen Rogers asked, knowing her twenty-five-year-old daughter better than she sometimes knew herself. "You know how your dad watches the weather. Kansas City had the same storm we did two weeks ago, and more snow is on the way. You shouldn't be driving and talking at the same time."

"The commute home is the only time I *could* call," Beth apologized, hating that she'd worried her mother. "You're already in your pajamas, aren't you? I didn't want to startle you awake with the phone ringing at midnight just to tell you my holiday schedule had changed. You'd think it was some kind of emergency."

The Jeep bumped over the corrugated ruts of snow that had fallen, melted and fallen again over the past two weeks as Beth made another, safer, turn. There were a lot of benefits to being a single woman owning her first home—the independence to come and go as she pleased, the freedom to decorate it any way she liked, building up the personal equity. But there were downfalls, too. Shoveling her own sidewalks and driveway at 11:47 p.m. topped that list right about now. Because two more inches of sleety crystals had fallen earlier in the evening, she'd better resign herself to taking a few minutes after unloading her groceries to at least salt the front walk so the mail carrier didn't trip the light fantastic tomorrow.

Not wanting to whine about even the tiniest thing for fear that her parents would fret even more about her decision to move to K.C. after small-town life and an old boyfriend had left her wanting something more, Beth went on with her explanation for the late-night call. "Dr. Landon is under a lot of pressure from the board of directors right now, and he needs me to put in some extra hours. It was too impersonal to send an e-mail to tell you how sorry I am that I'll have to cut short my trip home. I know that Jesse is home from college and that Frank and his wife and the kids will be there."

Her mother confirmed that both brothers would be at the farm for the holidays, while Beth spent most of her December at the office. "You don't have to apologize. I understand what it's like to be low woman on the totem pole, so that it's hard to get vacation time. But surely your office closes for a few days? I mean, who sells drugs on Christmas?"

Beth laughed. "That's what the college degree was for, Mom. I'm in management now. Not retail. People get sick 365 days a year, so GlennCo is producing goods somewhere in the world around the clock. That's a lot of employees and a lot of product to coordinate. It's up to people like Dr. Landon and me to make sure all those worldwide connections run smoothly so that you can walk into a pharmacy or check into a hospital or care facility and get exactly what you need to get well—"

"—even if it's Christmas." Beth's parents had always made her feel proud of her accomplishments. "Of course, your father and I want you to honor your commitments. We'll just make the most of the time you *are* here, and then maybe you can drive down to Fulton and stay for a week or so in the spring—or whenever you've built up the vacation time and the company can spare you."

Beth smiled. "Sounds like a plan."

"Stay warm. We love you."

"Love you, too, Mom. Give Dad a hug for me, too."

"I will."

Once her mother had hung up, Beth set

her phone on the passenger seat and turned onto her street. As was typical for the suburban neighborhood on a Monday night, the houses were already closed up as it approached 12:00 a.m. Cars were parked and silent, windows were dark.

The one exception was her new neighbor—new as of yesterday, in fact. A light was shining through the slits on either side of the faded, holey blanket masking his front porch window. He was probably still up late unpacking boxes after work. Although she'd seen three or four strapping, good-looking men hauling a bed and what little furniture would fit in the back of a pickup truck yesterday morning, she hadn't had the chance to introduce herself yet. In fact, she hadn't even been home long enough to find out which of the men had actually moved in.

Beth grinned with amusement as she drove past the blue-and-white bungalow house. She could guess that her mysterious new neighbor was single and male—either recently divorced or a confirmed bachelor—if the lack of furniture and tattered, makeshift window covering were any indication.

Her smile widened as she turned into her

driveway. Someone had already cleared her drive and front walk. "Thanks, Hank."

She glanced into her rearview mirror at the older house across the street. Her newest friend, Hank Whitaker, was a sweet septuagenarian widower with white hair who seemed to delight in looking out for her. Saturday morning, he'd been bragging about buying a new electric snow blower to replace his older, gas-powered model. Beth had no doubts that Hank had spent the evening clearing the sidewalks all the way down to the end of the block, just to test out his new toy. There were definitely some home-baked cookies and a personal thank-you in his future.

Beth pressed the automatic garage-door opener and pulled inside. Now she could put away the groceries and even have time for a hot bath and a few minutes to read before she went to bed.

After killing the engine and closing the garage door, she reached for her purse and leather attaché bag and looped them both over her shoulder. She got out and opened the back hatch of the Jeep, groaning when she saw the tumble of oranges, yogurt cups and soup cans that had rolled out of the bags—probably when she'd whipped around that corner earlier. She collected the goodies and restuffed the canvas bags, hooking the handles over her left wrist before closing the rear door and window. She was on her way to the wood stairs leading up to the kitchen door when she spotted her cell phone sitting inside on the car seat.

Beth shook her head. "I need another hand."

At this rate, by the time she finally got everything inside, she'd have to skip the bath. Still, if she wanted to charge her phone…

Sliding everything up onto her shoulders, she opened the door and picked up her cell phone. A leather strap caught on the door when she tried to close it. Lurching to avoid strangling herself, the grocery bags thunked down to the bend of her elbow, pulling her farther off balance. Muttering the kind of curse her mother would frown upon, Beth stuck the phone between her teeth, shouldered her purse and attaché, clutched the bags up against her chest and butted the door shut with her hip. Then, in a feat of straightforward determination, she shimmied between the Jeep and garage wall up to the kitchen door.

Thank God she never locked the thing. Turning the knob with her hands full would be tricky enough. Finding her keys in a pocket at this point would mean…what was that drumming sound?

The door burst open, smacking Elisabeth in the shoulder and knocking her off the stairs. "What the…?"

A dark figure in a stocking mask stormed through the opening, his white teeth snarling through the opening of his mask. Big hands clamped onto her arms and lifted her off her feet, shoving her aside like a lineman clearing the field for a running back.

Groceries flew. The front grill of the Jeep swirled through her vision. Her startled yelp of protest ended abruptly as she hit the concrete floor. The walls crashed and clattered down around her. The dark figure loomed over her like a shadow. Something smacked down hard against the side of her head. A sharp pain swirled through her skull, spinning her world into darkness.

IT COULD HAVE BEEN SECONDS or minutes later when Elisabeth opened her eyes again. When she blinked away the white dots of light swirling through her vision, she instantly knew three things.

She was alone in the garage.

Her coat, suit jacket and blouse had been unbuttoned.

And her head hurt like hell.

But it wasn't throbbing so badly that she couldn't think. *Call 9-1-1,* her brain shouted. "Call 9-1-1," she whispered through trembling lips.

Her body jolted at the slam of a door, sending a twinge of pain through her shoulder and hip. Inside? Outside? The man in the black mask might have gone back into the house. He might not be the only intruder there.

She needed to make that call.

Rolling onto her back was enough to make her dizzy. But even as she squeezed her eyes shut and waited for the queasy response in her stomach to pass, she patted her coat pockets. They'd been emptied out. Her skin crawled with the awareness that the stranger had touched her clothes, touched her. Ignoring the creepy sense of violation, Elisabeth ran her hands along her body and the floor beside her. Beyond the aches and heaviness of her head, she seemed to be unharmed. Her quick inspection discovered bruises, one glove and a tin of mints, but no phone.

Gritting her teeth against the ball bearings pinging from one side of her skull to the other, Elisabeth got her hands beneath her and pushed herself up to a sitting position. She spotted the contents of her purse, scattered through the shadows, and forced herself onto her hands and knees to search for her phone. Oh, no. She'd had her phone wedged between her teeth before they'd both sailed through the air. She squinted to see if she could spot it underneath her car or behind the bike and snow shovel she must have knocked over when she fell. But it was too dark to see and too hard to focus.

The icy temperature of the concrete floor seeped into her palms and through the wool of her gray slacks, rousing her enough to make her realize she was crawling toward the open kitchen door. The door to her back yard was standing wide open, as well.

What if she had passed out for only a few seconds? The garage might be stone-cold quiet, but who knew what waited for her inside the house? Another burglar? Something worse?

"Get out," she muttered, grabbing on to the bumper of her Jeep and pulling herself up.

Go.

Kicking aside groceries and the items from her purse, Beth staggered to the wall and punched in the code to open her garage door again. The grinding noise of the rising door grated against her ears and spurred her uneven footsteps. If the man—or men—were still here, they'd hear her escape.

Hurry!

As soon as she made it outside, the blast of damp winter air chapped her cheeks and chest, and eased the foggy disconnect in her brain. She needed to get someplace safe.

Now!

Calling to her like a beacon in the night, she turned toward the one lighted window on her street. Clasping her blouse and jacket together at her neck, she stepped knee-deep into the snow and cut straight across the yard to her neighbor's house. She stumbled once. But the icy moisture that sank into her cleavage and dribbled down to the exposed skin at her waist cleared away the last of her dizziness, leaving fear and pulse-pumping adrenaline in its place.

She wasn't safe.

She needed to be safe.

Beth jogged the last few yards—climbed the front steps onto the noisy planks of the porch. "Hello?" She knocked on the storm door. "Hel—"

She was answered by a loud woof. Then there was a thump, and a thunderous alarm like stampeding hooves charged the opposite side of the door.

Beth clutched her fist over the frantic pounding of her heart. "Oh, my God."

The growling, ferocious bark of the dog inside the house jerked her back a step. When the inside door rattled, she imagined the beast flinging its full weight against it. Hugging her arms more tightly around herself, she retreated until her shoulders pressed against one of the porch's wood pillars. A cloud of her own shaky breaths in the frozen air fogged her vision.

What should she do? Where could she go?

Glancing over to the gaping mouth of her open garage, Elisabeth quickly debated which danger she'd rather face. A man who'd violated her home and others who might be lying in wait to do her more harm? Or the vicious hound from hell, slavering and bellowing on the other side of that door? How had she missed seeing a dog—a guard dog… a mutant-size guard dog—moving in?

Elisabeth turned to the street and hugged the post. She could wake up Hank. But he'd have his hearing aids out, so it would take him forever to hear the doorbell and answer—allowing plenty of time for the intruder to track her down and finish what he'd started if that was his aim.

"Damn it, Beth, think," she ordered herself, haphazardly buttoning her wet blouse with fingers that were growing colder and stiffer by the minute.

A car door slammed, drawing her attention to the end of the street. Her heart raced with matching speed as an engine gunned. Clinging to the porch post, she squinted to see beyond the dim circles of illumination cast by the streetlights. The squeal of spinning tires, screaming to find traction on the icy pavement, pierced the thick, cold air. She could make out nothing more than the fact that it was a car, as black and blurry and impossible to identify as the man who'd attacked her. The vehicle spun around the corner onto the main road and disappeared from sight.

Nothing suspicious about that. Much. Like she was going back into her own house by herself now.

"What do you want?"

Elisabeth whirled around at the bass-deep voice behind her.

And screamed.

BETH SLAPPED HER HAND over her mouth, embarrassed that she could be so easily spooked. Embarrassed that instead of coming up with a proper greeting, begging for help or uttering an apology for waking him in the middle of the night, her first reaction to the height and bulk of the man in the shadows was to scream.

When had the door opened?

Where were the rest of his clothes?

And why the hell was he armed?

Instead of improving on her ability to communicate, the next words out of Beth's mouth were, "Don't shoot me."

He muttered something distinctly inelegant that triggered a bone-rattling woof from the dog behind the glass storm door.

Although the man lowered the black-barreled gun he held in his left hand, it did little to change her first impression that he was an ominous force to be reckoned with. Her new neighbor was eerily quiet, obviously irritated and quite possibly the biggest, broadest silhouette of a man she'd ever seen. Images of sci-fi monsters and Mack trucks leaped to mind.

"Were you in an accident? I heard a car pealing away."

It was difficult to hear his exact words over the dog's barking. But she felt the man speak. The deep timbre of his voice rumbled from his chest and skittered across her skin, raising goose bumps. Or maybe that was just the cold and wet finally soaking through all of her clothes.

She tore her gaze from the naked chest above his unsnapped jeans and nodded at the tank-size bundle of barking muscle bouncing up and down on the other side of the storm door's window. A big black nose, broad muzzle and sharp teeth were all she could make out. Elisabeth shrank back a step. "You're not going to let the dog out, are you?"

She jerked back another step when the man pounded the doorframe with his fist.

"Daisy. Room."

Daisy? Who named a monster Daisy? With an almost disappointed whimper, the dog turned and trotted away into the interior of the darkened house, its crooked, scraggly tail wagging behind her.

Elisabeth's pulse still thundered in her ears. "I'm sorry I…" *screamed in your face* "…woke you." That would account for the bare feet and lack of a shirt.

But not the gun.

Big man. Big gun. Woman alone. Bad idea.

She retreated farther, hoping her smile didn't look as forced as it felt. "I didn't mean to disturb you. Or…D-Daisy. I saw your light on upstairs and thought you were still awake."

"Stop."

She thumbed over her shoulder. "No, really. I'll go over to Hank's across the street. He knows me—"

He moved from the shadows. A viselike hand snaked around her wrist. "I said *stop*."

"*You* stop." Instinctively, Beth fought against the unexpected touch. "Let go of me!"

"You're about to fall off the top step," he

groused, effortlessly tugging her off her feet and dragging her toward him.

She stumbled into the middle of his chest, her palm bracing against a swell of hard muscle and crisp hair a split-second before her nose hit the fragrant spot. Singed by the damp heat that clung to his hair and skin, she snatched her fingers away. With the same grip on her wrist he quickly righted her and released her as soon as she regained her balance.

"Why didn't you just say so?" She felt a little foolish at her fight-or-flight response, and more than a little pissed that her crazy weird day had deteriorated down to a midnight wrestle she couldn't hope to win with a man she didn't even know. She was scared; she was tired. It was freaking cold. Her head throbbed, and, damn it, she just wanted to use his phone! "I'm sorry to welcome you to the neighborhood this way, but would it kill you to turn on a light or chain up your dog? Or announce it before you grab someone and scare the crap out of them? I just wanted to borrow your phone to call the police!"

With another terse grumble that seemed to be directed more at himself than at her, he tucked the gun into the back of his jeans and reached inside the door to flip a switch. Beth squeezed her eyes shut as the light beside the door came on, and even its meager light blazed into her retinas. "Happy now?"

In the few seconds it took to blink her eyes open and let them adjust to the light, her goliath of a neighbor flipped a leather wallet on a chain looped around his neck, drawing her attention to the flash of color there. The brass-and-blue enamel badge seemed out of place, hanging against the T of dark gold hair that sprinkled from pec to pec—save for the void of a puckered, circular scar near his left shoulder— and narrowed down to a thin line that disappeared behind the open snap of his jeans.

"You…*you're* the police?" she stuttered. Not another bad guy? Not the Terminator-next-door?

"Detective Kevin Grove, KCPD." He scanned her with a quick thoroughness from head to toe and back, hunching down to give her eyes another look. "You're that woman from next door."

"I'm Beth…Elisabeth Rogers."

"We've got the amenities out of the way. Now what the hell is going on?"

Her first, frightening impression of him in

the shadows hadn't been far off. The straight-on glimpse into his face gave her a chance to identify that the knot on the bridge of his crooked nose, which marked where it had once been broken, was real. Just as real were the aggressively square jaw and sharp cheek-bones that stretched taut beneath a scratchy stubble of sandy-colored beard. His hair was clipped short, and stood up in damp, dark gold spikes across the top of his head. If his eyes had been cold glass instead of a rich amber brown, she might have thought him some kind of futuristic cyborg, created to hunt and destroy—sculpted to be functional, not handsome.

The instant she took in his intimidating features, he frowned, deepening the grooves beside his mouth. "Why do you need a cop?" He straightened to well over six feet, proving that standing a head taller barefoot than she did in a pair of boots hadn't been a trick of her imagination, either.

Embarrassed to be caught staring at his harsh features, yet equally fascinated by the rugged hills and hollows of his chest and arms, she could only point across the yard. "There was a man…"

"In your house?" He crossed to the railing, his gaze tracking the direction of her finger. It was too overcast for the snow to reflect much light, but something seemed to have caught his eye.

"Yes."

"That was him driving off?" He circled around her to the edge of the porch and knelt down to inspect some dots of paint on the top step.

"I'm not sure." Elisabeth turned to see if she could spot what his night-vision eyes apparently had, feeling only marginally safer to know he had a badge to justify that gun, and that his size and strength and grouchy demeanor were used for the forces of good, not evil. "He had a stocking mask on over his face."

"Do you remember anything about his height? His build?"

"It happened so fast. He shoved me down. I don't know what I hit—maybe just the garage floor. I couldn't find my cell phone and I was afraid to go inside—"

"That was smart." He seemed intent on whatever he was rubbing between his thumb and fingers, making the praise sound rote and insincere. "Tell me more."

Instead of replaying the attack in her head, her attention was drawn to the broad back that tapered down to a strip of black elastic and the gun peeking out above the waistband of his unbelted jeans. Had she gotten him out of bed and he'd pulled on his jeans over a pair of briefs? She was shivering beneath several layers of wool and cotton, but there was a sheen of dampness at the small of his back. He was barefoot, too. Just the jeans and briefs and gun despite the bitter chill. Had she pulled him from a late-night shower?

At the first knock, the first bark, he must have shut off the water, grabbed his gun and badge and a pair of pants and come running. Imagining the whole bulk of him completely naked…. That was one hell of a lot of man. Right there. Within arm's reach. If she could just…one touch…

Her breath caught and her vision blurred as she curled her fingers into her palm and tucked them deep into the pockets of her coat. More weirdness. This was so not the time for any feminine curiosity to kick in. He was too big, too fierce-looking, to be attractive. And yet…With an embarrassingly breathless gasp, she forced herself to focus her thoughts and tear her gaze from that mesmerizing strip of black elastic. Man in her house, remember? Attacked? *Concentrate*.

They'd been rough hands. Invasive hands that had opened her coat and touched her while she'd been out. Far more damaging than Detective Grove's grip had been. "He wore a black wool pea coat. Leather gloves. And he…he…"

"Ah, hell." He was rising, turning. Advancing.

Beth trembled inside her clothes and backed away as he reached for her again. She swatted his hand away. "What is it?"

"You."

"Me?"

He pointed to her face and she finally made sense of what had caught his eye. Ruby red drops on her coat sleeve. More, in the footprints she'd left on his front walk. Blood. Trailing a path across the snow to her garage door.

Her blood.

"Oh, my God."

Beth put her fingers to her left temple and felt the warm stickiness in her hair. Her knees turned to jelly. The white planks of the porch rushed up to meet her.

But she never hit the painted wood. Steel bands caught her behind her shoulders and beneath her knees. Her cheek tumbled against a furnace of heat that was solid and deliciously fragrant—like spice and musk and man.

Man?

A ripple of panic tried to rouse her. He was holding her. They were moving. Beth flattened her palms against the wall of her neighbor's chest and pushed. But she had no strength. "What are you doing? Put me down, you big brute."

"No passing out on my front porch, okay, lady?" His dark eyes locked onto hers. "Sorry I didn't explain the rules before I grabbed you."

The mysterious detective with the gruff sarcasm and villainous looks locked her in his arms and carried her inside the house as Beth's world faded to black.

Chapter Two

"Call in a uniform to secure the scene ASAP." The blur of city lights raced past the windows of Detective Kevin Grove's silver SUV. "Hold on."

A spray of chopped-up ice and slush coated his windshield as he swerved into the passing lane to avoid a slow-moving snowplow. With a curse, he paused the conversation to turn on his windshield wipers and flicked up his high-beams to see through the messy, nearly deserted streets. Once he'd swung onto the boulevard that would take him to the Truman Medical Center, he shifted his attention back to the phone clipped to his ear.

His words were concise as he relayed his orders and his new home address to the KCPD dispatcher. "It's the ranch-style house just to the north of my place. I'm en route to the hospital with the victim, but I'll have my phone on if the officer on the scene has any questions. Tell whoever's responding to get me a printout of any other burglaries or vandalism reports in the neighborhood for the past few months. As soon as I deliver Ms. Rogers, I'll be back to go over the house myself. I want to assess the break-in more thoroughly."

"I told you I could get myself to the E.R.," the drowsy female voice murmured from the passenger seat across from him. *Yeah, like Sleeping Beauty over there had any business getting behind the wheel of a car tonight.* "If you would have let me use your phone to call 9-1-1 like I'd asked, you could be sleeping right now. I'm not trying to be an imposition."

Beth Rogers's apology was logical and kind, and Kevin warned every bone in his body to ignore the soft words.

"Your skin was like ice and you were bleeding on my couch. I wasn't going to wait."

Kevin had trained himself to turn a cold shoulder to damsels in distress. It was the curse of a bulldog-ugly face and a battered heart that had paid a dear price for confusing need with caring. *Don't get involved. Don't give a damn. Don't get hurt.* He'd been burned once too often—by a mother who hadn't wanted him, yet who'd paid dramatic surprise visits in and out of his life over the years, demanding his money, his connections or his big shoulder to cry on when the world hadn't gone her way. And he'd been burned once too well—by a seductive witch who'd taken the best he had to give before walking away.

He was smart to be cautious.

But a dazed beauty leaving a trail of blood in the snow? Footprints, too big to be hers, across the patio behind her house? Jimmied hinges ripped from the wood on the French doors that showed where an intruder had forced his way inside her home?

Those were details that the cop in him couldn't ignore. Even his cursory investigation when he'd gone to retrieve her purse and ID had given him enough reason to suspect that the crime—whatever she had interrupted—was real enough. A knight in shining armor he refused to be. Ever again. But a cop?

Until his dying breath.

"Get a CSI team over there to see if they can find anything to ID the intruder. Grove out." He tapped the phone and disconnected the call.

Kevin spared a glance for the woman nodding off in the passenger seat across from him. Those gray-blue eyes were drifting shut again, brushing dark lashes over her pale, softly freckled cheeks.

"Come on, lady. Wake up." Ignoring his command, she snuggled deeper against the SUV's gray upholstery. He cranked the heater up another notch, praying it was the late hour and not shock or something worse that was making her too fatigued to respond. "Hey!"

She groaned in response—a soft, throaty sound that beat at his conscience and tried to wriggle beneath his resolve to feel nothing.

The proverbial girl-next-door looked about sixteen curled up across the seat, with just the fringe of her mink-colored hair showing beneath the black knit watch cap he'd pulled onto her head. The cap was meant to hold a clean dish towel in place over the gash at her temple. But the dimensions of the cap, sized to fit his head, made her look fragile and small. Yet he knew from cradling her in his arms that she was no child. He knew from laying her on his couch to check for other injuries while the dizzy spell passed that she had fit, strong legs about a mile long, no-nonsense hands used to work—not to make a fashion statement— and healthy curves in all the right places. Her driver's license said she was twelve years younger than his thirty-seven, but he'd discovered the tiniest of laugh lines beside her eyes and mouth. Despite the ethereal dusting of freckles and the elfin haircut, Beth Rogers was all grown woman. And her womanly scent, an enticing combination of sweetness and spice, was filling up the SUV's interior and imprinting itself like a familiar memory into his brain.

Those kinds of details he shouldn't be noticing.

Kevin pressed on the accelerator, cruising through an intersection as the light turned red. He had the siren going, his lights flashing and a gut-deep motivation to get his injured neighbor to the hospital—to personally make sure she was in safe hands so he wouldn't suffer a guilty conscience for turning her back out of his life come morning.

So much for solitude. He'd left his apartment in downtown K.C. to find a place with a yard for his rescue mutt, Daisy, to run in, and some peace and quiet for him to get away from this kind of crap. He hadn't been in the place forty-eight hours, hadn't even unpacked the boxes he'd hauled in, before his job—and a woman in need—had come pounding on his front door, demanding his attention.

He should be relaxing in a hot shower and washing off the paint from the trim work he'd tackled after his shift downtown had ended. Instead, he was playing a reluctant Sir Galahad to a woman he didn't know—a woman whose sympathetic squint when she'd gotten a good look at him in the light had given him a truer reading of her first impression of him than her startled scream had. All the more reason to drive her to the hospital himself and leave her someplace safe. Someplace where *he* wouldn't feel as though it was his personal duty to take care of her. He had no room for *personal* in his life. Not anymore.

He'd do his job by Freckles over there—nobody had better question his skills or professionalism on that count ever again. But he'd answered enough false alarms with Sheila last summer. He'd paid dearly for caring—for answering the call of duty with more than his badge. He wouldn't be duped by a pretty face again.

Not even if the blood on that face was real.

Kevin slowed his speed before reaching across the seat. He squeezed Beth's shoulder through the thick wool of her chocolate-brown coat. "Come on, lady. Wake up."

The dark lashes fluttered. Hell. He gave her a slight shake. "No passing out on me, remember?"

Peachy, unadorned lips moved as she squirmed out of his grasp. "I'm awake."

"I need to see your eyes, okay?"

The muted blue eyes blinked open, focused for a moment on his ugly mug, then closed again. "You're bossy. *And* you're speeding."

Kevin resolutely stiffened the muscles that wanted to grin and put both hands back on the wheel. Good. A smart mouth required thinking. Thinking required her head to be in fairly good working order. Even though he was no medic, he'd had enough first-aid training to know that the two-inch gash at her temple needed stitches. But it was the fainting spell and possible concussion that had him worried the most.

"Come on, Sleeping Beauty. I can't watch you and the road at the same time. I need you to talk to me."

Her weary sigh whispered across his eardrums. "Like I said, *bossy*. What do you want to talk about?"

"Tell me everything you remember about the break-in."

"Haven't we already had that conversation?"

"You're thinking more clearly now. Maybe I'll get some coherent answers out of you."

The gray-blue eyes opened to half mast and seemed to fix somewhere in the vicinity of his shoulder. "I was in my garage, juggling groceries and stuff from work, heading into the kitchen when the door opened. The man was already in the house. He threw me out of his way and the lights went out. Next thing I knew, I was booking it over to your place."

"He *threw* you? You mean he physically picked you up and tossed you aside?"

She seemed to be reliving the memory, staring down at the fingers twisting in her lap, before she nodded. "Yeah. I flew halfway across my garage."

Although he'd carried her into his living room easily enough, Beth Rogers was no featherweight. It would take someone with considerable strength to propel a grown woman through the air.

When her gaze darted across the seat to him, he knew she was thinking the same thing. *He'd* be strong enough to do something like that.

Well, hell. Kevin tightened his grip on the steering wheel, fighting the urge to argue that he would never—that he *had* never, despite one vengeful woman's claim to the contrary— use his superior strength against an innocent lady. *Be a cop,* he reminded his emotions. *Don't get angry. Don't be defensive. Don't care.* If Beth Rogers was frightened away from any kind of neighborly acquaintance beyond tonight's emergency because of his appearance and attitude, so much the better for his privacy and peace of mind.

"So you never went inside?" the cop in him asked.

"Nope."

"Did he say anything?"

"No, he just…"

If her skin could get any paler, it just did. She wasn't passing out on him again, was she? "He just what?"

"He started to undress me." Her fingers stopped their frenetic wrangling and squeezed into fists. "Maybe I wasn't unconscious for as long as I thought. Coming to must have scared him away from doing anything…horrible…to me."

Ah, hell. Double hell. "That *didn't* happen," he insisted. Kevin reached across the seat and covered both of her hands with his. Her startled gasp matched his own surprise at how unplanned, how presumptuous the move had been.

In the time it took for the lingering chill of her soft skin to register, he was pulling away, firmly wrapping his fingers back around the wheel and silently cursing his inability to focus on the job he was supposed to do.

"Sorry, you just startled…" Her fingers fluttered after his, as though she wanted to reclaim his hand. But it must have been a trick of his imagination because she tucked them just as quickly back into her lap. "Why would he do that?"

"Do you have any enemies?" Kevin asked. "A jealous boyfriend? Any dangerous habits, like drugs or gambling?"

Kevin felt her eyes open wide. He glanced across the seat to find her gaze staring straight into his.

"No." The frown on her lips indicated that his questions had offended her. Or frightened her. Or struck a nerve. "I've lived in Kansas City only a few months. I work at GlennCo Pharmaceuticals from 9:00 a.m. to 6:00 p.m. or later on most days—not counting the commute. When I'm off, I'm fixing up my house—or, this time of year, working on Christmas projects or shopping. There's no time for a boyfriend and no budget for any *dangerous* habits."

"You come home this late by yourself every night?" The clock on the dashboard read well past midnight. "A woman alone? A familiar routine? The perverts of the world don't need any better setup than that to commit a crime."

Beth hugged her arms around her middle and turned her focus straight forward through the windshield. "Please tell me this was just a burglary that I interrupted."

"I can't say."

"You can't say?"

He wouldn't give her words he didn't know to be true. "I won't confirm any suspicions until I've done a little more investigating."

"That's annoyingly mysterious. How about, 'I'm looking into it. Don't worry. It'll be okay'?"

"I won't promise something I don't know for a fact." He killed the siren and tapped on the brake to slow the SUV as the bright lights of the Truman Medical Center parking lot came into view. "We're here."

She sat up straighter in her seat, gingerly pushing the edges of the knit cap and dish towel from her eyes. "What kind of cop are you, anyway? Besides the bossy, pessimistic kind."

"I'm a master detective with the major case squad at KCPD." Kevin pulled into a parking spot just beyond the emergency room's circular drive. He turned off the engine and got out.

By the time he'd circled around the hood and opened the passenger door to help her out, Beth had unbuckled and twisted to face him. She clasped her coat together beneath her chin and blinked against the spit of frozen moisture in the air. "Major case means you solve murders and kidnappings and other really serious crimes, right?"

He hooked a hand beneath her elbow and steadied her as she climbed down. "Yeah."

"I guess my little bump on the head is beneath you."

Kevin kept a grip on her elbow and short-ened his stride so that she could walk through the sliding emergency-room doors beside him.

"A cop is a cop." He guided her straight over to the check-in desk and got in line behind a woman holding a wailing, red-faced toddler. "It's not what I had planned for the night. But it's no waste of time if a real crime has been committed."

With an unexpected burst of temper, Freckles tugged her arm from his grip. "*If?* You think I'm making this up? That I did this to myself?"

"Don't twist my words around, lady." A sharp look from the woman in front of them toned down his response to a glare and a whisper. "You needed help—I helped. I'll get your report to the right department at KCPD. I wasn't insinuating anything."

"Could have fooled me. You've made me feel like a nuisance all night long." Pressing a hand to the wound on her head, Freckles tipped her head back and returned the glare full force. "And I have a name, Detective. You can call me Elisabeth, or Beth or even Miss Rogers. But don't keep referring to me as 'lady.' In fact, you don't have to refer to me at all. Thank you for the ride. Sorry I ruined your plans, upset your dog and forced you to leave home. I absolve you of all responsibility for me. Good night."

"You didn't force me to…"

Kevin bit his tongue as a nurse came up to the woman and child to lead them down the hallway. Before he could finish the argument, Beth Rogers scooted in front of him and handed her insurance card over the counter to the young male clerk behind the desk. Her stiff shoulders and full back made her aversion to his continued *brutish, bossy, pessimistic* presence crystal clear.

This was what he wanted, right? Scare away any relationship that might turn remotely personal, that might get him into trouble again? Sheila had triggered his protective instincts at her first late-night phone call that spring, claiming she had a stalker outside her apartment door. Kevin had broken speed records getting across town to rescue her. By the end of summer, she'd proven him a sap of the worst order. What he'd called love, she'd called a working partnership. An attorney, she'd used him to get information that her law firm had used to help a client walk on a case KCPD had built against him. What Kevin had defended as a relationship betrayed, Sheila claimed was sexual harassment—that he'd forced her into something more personal.

And even though he'd been cleared of the accusation, the stigma stuck. Kevin Grove was a fool when it came to women. A big, ugly-ass fool who had no business playing hero to any woman. Not Sheila Mercer. And not Beth Rogers.

He should be relieved that his next-door neighbor had had enough of his company. There'd be no chance that he'd make the same mistake twice.

Dismissing her with a scowl, he turned toward the exit doors. "Good night."

KEVIN SAT IN THE PARKING lot—in the night, in the cold—for thirty minutes, waging a war between his conscience and self-preservation. He'd done right by Miss Elisabeth Rogers—gotten her to the hospital, called in the break-in, listened to her report. As a cop, he was square with her.

As a man…? His self-deprecating sigh clouded the air inside the SUV. Her freckled, alabaster skin—that could blush with temper or go pale with pain and fear—had gotten beneath his own tough hide somehow. He couldn't just drive off and leave her alone, even though she was in safe hands now, could he? That lecturing, accusatory tongue indicated she could take care of herself. But a woman who was frightened enough, desperate enough to want to hold on to him—however briefly—was either a nut case…or in serious need of an ally right about now.

And he'd hate to think a face that was so all-American pretty could be hiding a crazy lady inside.

Still, it took an ambulance pulling up and the attendants wheeling out a fragile, white-haired old woman hooked up to an IV and an oxygen mask before his conscience finally won out over his damned pride and wounded heart. If he didn't stand up for the underdogs of this world, protect those who'd been preyed upon, then what was the point of being such a big, bad bruiser of a man, anyway?

His Grandma Miriam had always said there was a purpose for him in this world. She'd given him love and had raised him when no one else wanted the job. No bigger than a minute, she was the one person in this world who could make him give a damn about things when he didn't want to. Thoughts of Miriam, and the frail patient who reminded him of her, pushed Kevin back out into the cold night.

He hadn't done right by the half-dressed, terrified woman on his doorstep tonight, after all. Not yet.

Inhaling a lungful of bracing air, he walked back inside the hospital. He flashed his badge at the young man behind the check-in counter. "Where's the lady I brought in here a little while ago? Elisabeth Rogers?"

The clerk checked a chart on his desk. "Trauma Room 3. Dr. Rodriguez-Grant is working on her…sir?"

But Kevin was already striding down the

hallway. The woman could damn well be an imposition on his solitude, a threat to his hormones. But he wasn't going to have Grandma Miriam's voice stuck in his head, telling him how disappointed she was that he couldn't set aside his own pain and distrust to help a woman when she needed him most.

He burst through the swinging door with a number 3 on it. Oh, yeah. He'd have been toast the next time he visited Miriam if he hadn't seen this job all the way through to the end.

He *was* toast.

Beth Rogers's gray-blue gaze widened with surprise and locked onto his.

There were no tricks of shadows or frosty air to mask the injuries of the woman sitting up on the hospital bed. In the bright light of the treatment room, a purplish-red swelling stood out in startling contrast against her pale cheek. Matching bruises in the pattern of thumb and fingerprints—the span of a man's hand—dappled her bare shoulder where the white hospital gown she wore draped loosely. A woman doctor with a long, dark pony-tail was taping a gauze bandage over the row of neat stitches at Beth's left temple.

An angry bubble of emotion stuck in

Kevin's throat. And he'd been beastly enough to worry about protecting himself? He had to swallow hard before he could speak. "You all right?"

But the dark-haired woman had no trouble with words. She set her scissors on a tray and faced him. "This is a private room, sir. I'm going to have to ask you to leave."

It took a second for Kevin to tear his gaze from Beth, read Dr. Emilia Rodriguez-Grant's name tag and remember to pull his badge from beneath his coat. "Kevin Grove, KCPD. I brought the patient in."

The doctor glanced over her shoulder at Beth, sized up Kevin one more time then spoke to her patient again. "Are you okay with him being here?"

There was no way to miss the implication of the doctor's light touch against the bruises on Beth's shoulder, no way to miss the direct look into Beth's eyes. Dr. Rodriguez-Grant suspected abuse. She suspected *him*.

Well, hell. His anger, however misinterpreted, already filled the room. How was he supposed to defend himself without coming across like the bullying SOB she suspected him to be? Kevin scraped his palm over his stubbly jaw, wishing he could mold a kinder, gentler expression onto his features, but knowing he'd have to rely on a mixture of logic and calm instead to convince the doctor of his innocence.

He needn't have bothered.

"*He* didn't do this to me." With a strength of tone that belied her battered body, Beth Rogers thrust out her hand. She reached for him, summoned him to cross the sterile room to stand beside her. "Detective Grove is a…neighbor." When he didn't go so far as to take the offered hand, she pulled his hand from his side. Her fingers tapped against his palm before lightly closing around his, revealing that she was a little more hesitant to defend the big beast than her outward attitude might claim. "He was kind enough to help me out tonight. He drove me into town."

"So you reported the assault?" Dr. Rodriguez-Grant asked, making no bones about visually evaluating her patient's comfort level with Kevin hovering so close by.

"Yes," Beth answered. "To him."

Kevin's response was more certain. "I'll need a copy of Miss Rogers's medical report

to put with the file I'm setting up at KCPD."
Already discomfited by how easy it was to
keep hold of her hand, he wisely let go so he
could pull a business card from his wallet and
hand it to the doctor. "You can send it to me
here."

"I know the address. My brother and
husband are both cops."

Kevin grinned as she tucked the card into
the pocket of her lab coat. Dr. Rodriguez-
Grant wasn't completely sold on him yet. He
had no doubt she'd be checking up on him.
"Yeah? You know A. J. Rodriguez?"

She nodded. "That'd be big brother."

Kevin knew the name, knew the reputa-
tion. If thoroughness was a family trait, then
Beth had been well taken care of. "I've
worked with A.J. on a few cases."

Her dark eyes softened just a bit before she
moved her tray to a side counter and placed
a syringe in the safe disposal unit on the wall
above it. "I'm married to Justin Grant—a
bomb-squad specialist. Elisabeth, I'll run up
and check your film for a fracture or any other
abnormalities, although your responses
indicate there's nothing to worry about. Better
safe than sorry, though. Detective."

He nodded as she left the room. "Doc." He followed her to the door, making sure the doctor was out of earshot before he turned to face Beth. "You didn't have to do that."

"Your attack-dog approach to meeting new people gives a lousy first impression. She thought you were the one who hurt me."

"I know."

"Doesn't it make you mad that someone assumes that about you?"

"You think I can't take care of myself?"

With a huffy sigh, she pulled her gown back into place and drew her knees up to hug her arms around them. "I thought we were done trying to be friends, that I'd taxed the limits of your ability to be civil. Why did you come back?"

"My grandmother."

"Huh?"

"Don't ask." Pulling back the front edges of his tan wool coat, Kevin propped his hands at the waist of his jeans. "Do you have any family I can call for you so you're not here by yourself?"

"Guilty conscience?"

"Just answer the question."

She tucked a wisp of mink-colored hair

behind her ear. "They live two and a half hours away in Fulton. Dr. Rodriguez-Grant says it's just a mild concussion—no internal bleeding. I don't want to worry Mom and Dad. They're stressed enough about me being on my own in the big city."

"You're a grown woman, aren't you?"

Her lips crooked with a wry smile. "They still worry. My younger brother lives with them, the older on the farm next door. So far, I'm the only one adventurous enough to leave home."

So she had no family here to lean on. "What about a friend? Or boyfriend?"

"No time for that, remember? The only people I've gotten to know are coworkers, and Hank across the street from us. He'll be dead to the world until he puts in his hearing aids in the morning. And I don't think I want you to call my boss over a bump on the head."

"That was way more than a bump on the head. So who's coming to take you home?"

"I'm not your problem anymore. I'm sure you have work in the morning and I don't know how much longer this will take. You don't need to stay."

"Who will you call?"

"Bossy *and* persistent." She shrugged. "I guess I'll call a cab."

"Kevin Elijah Grove." Miriam's quavery voice echoed inside his head. *"Always do the right thing, son. Even if it's hard. Serve your purpose. Be a man."*

Kevin silenced the voice by pulling off his coat and planting his butt on the stool in the corner of Beth Rogers's room. "Lady, I'm staying."

Chapter Three

"Thank you, Officer…Taylor?" Beth quickly hid her confused frown as the compactly built, uniformed officer who'd just hammered a pair of two-by-fours over her busted back doors turned to face her.

The dark-eyed Latino cop zipped up the front of his leather jacket and grinned. "I get that look a lot, ma'am." He winked. "I'm adopted."

"Oh."

"That plastic tarp I pulled from your garage ought to keep the worst of the cold out. Hope that was all right."

"That's fine." Exhausted as she was, it was easy to match the young officer's smile. "Thank you for making the place habitable until I can get to a hardware store tomorrow. Later today, I guess."

"No problem, ma'am."

Beth stood rooted to the spot as Officer Taylor crossed to the countertop bar between her kitchen and dining room to pack his hammer and leftover nails in the toolbox he'd brought in from his police cruiser. Despite the damage to her French doors and her own body, the motive for her attack remained unclear. Taylor, who'd been watching the crime scene since Kevin Grove had called it in, was of the opinion that her arrival had interrupted a burglary. Even though nothing appeared to be missing, he'd found her jewelry box emptied out on her bed at the far end of the house. And in her home office just across the hall from her bedroom, her computer tower had been disconnected from the monitor and knocked over, while the drawers of her desk had been pulled out and emptied into a mess on the floor. The television and sound system in her living room hadn't been touched. It was as if she'd come home just as the would-be thief's systematic room-to-room search had gotten under way. The lone CSI who'd come to the scene had taken pictures and dusted for prints, but, finding no one's fingerprints but hers, backed up Beth's recollection that the intruder had worn gloves.

In short, as crimes went, KCPD was of the opinion that Beth had dodged a bullet. Either through incompetence or poor timing, the man inside her house had stolen nothing more than her peace of mind.

To her way of thinking, it was violation enough. Along with her sense of security, her determination to strike out on her own and pursue a career and lifestyle her rural upbringing couldn't provide had been rattled.

The big, brooding presence of her reluctant rescuer had a lot to do with that unsettled feeling as well. While she appreciated Kevin Grove's thoroughness in giving her house and garage a personal inspection, there was something about the man that disturbed her equilibrium. Maybe it was the cold, matter-of-fact way he ordered the CSI to take the bloody shovel where she'd cut her head into the lab—to make sure it was the fall, and not the deliberate use as a weapon, that had put the six stitches in her head.

Maybe it was his abrasive lack of charm that he seemed to use to deliberately mask his better qualities—like refusing to leave her alone for the past four hours while she was injured and afraid, or personally inspecting every door and window on her house to make sure it'd be a damn sight harder to break in a second time. He was finally coming around to being a good neighbor—if not exactly what she'd call a friend. That was all she wanted, right?

Or maybe the uneasiness she felt at having Kevin Grove moving through her small home had more to do with her than with the man himself. Yes, the sheer bulk of him seemed to swallow up the space when he entered the room. Yes, his tough, busted-up features took some getting used to, and could never be called handsome. But there was something so indescribably masculine about his size, his scent, the depth of his voice, that it awakened something undeniably feminine in her. Beth barely knew him, yet she was quite certain that she'd never met anyone who was more man before.

Despite her headache, despite her fatigue, despite her misgivings about Kevin Grove—she jumped when the door to the garage swung open and the burly detective strode into her kitchen. He tossed the tape measure he carried to Officer Taylor, who caught it and dropped it into the toolbox before latching it shut.

Detective Grove nodded to the younger officer. "You were right. I measured about six feet from the bottom of the steps. Definitely not a fall."

Taylor nodded as he pulled on his black knit watch cap with the KCPD logo on the front—just like the borrowed one Beth had put back on over her own bandaged head. "It'd take a strong man to throw a person that far."

"Or someone with a lot of adrenaline pumping through him."

"You want me to put a general description on the wire?" Taylor asked. "There hasn't been any activity at the house or on the street in the couple hours I've been here. Not even a curious neighbor."

Because she was already the topic of conversation, Beth stepped forward to join the conversation. "Most of the people around here are retired. There are a couple of families with young children, too. So nobody keeps late hours, especially with all this snow and ice."

Detective Grove's dark amber gaze swung over to hers, perhaps finally understanding why, even though he'd been a stranger, she'd sought him out. They were the only two single, young adults on their block. As such, they were the only two people who'd been up so late. He was destined to be her savior tonight.

And as much as he aggravated her patience and pulse, she was grateful.

If Alex Taylor was aware of the silent communication going on between them, he didn't comment. Instead, he picked up his toolbox and headed for the front door. "I can hang around awhile longer, see if anybody who doesn't fit shows up in the neighborhood again."

Detective Grove followed him through the living room to dismiss him. "I imagine our perp is in the wind. I'll keep an eye on things tonight and take care of the paperwork in the morning."

"Very good, sir." The black-haired officer hesitated at the door. Like Beth, he had to tilt his head to look Grove in the eye. "I'll e-mail you my observations for your report, but I wanted to let you know that I'll be starting my SWAT training after Christmas. I expect you'll want to turn this break-in over to a uniform division, but you'll have to assign it to someone else. I'll be available as a consultant if they need me, though."

"I appreciate it." Maybe Beth shouldn't have been so surprised when Kevin Grove reached out to shake hands. While still snapping orders like a superior officer, he'd been far more talkative and friendly with his KCPD coworkers than he'd been with her. "You've got one hell of a family tradition to uphold, but I have no doubt you'll be a rock star at it. Good luck with SWAT, Alex."

"Thank you, sir." Alex Taylor nodded to Beth. "Good night, ma'am. Take care."

"Thanks again. Good night."

With a blast of wintry air, he walked out into the night. Kevin Grove pushed the door shut and turned to face Beth.

Now that it was just the two of them, the silence of the night outside crept in through every pore of the house. The detective pulled back the front of his knee-length wool coat and propped his hands on his hips in a stance that framed the badge hanging from his neck and gave her a glimpse of the gun holstered at his waist. He was all cop, all business, his scowling presence as unsettling as Officer Taylor's friendly demeanor had been reassuring. But nothing could be as unsettling as things were about to get once he followed Officer Taylor out the door and left her alone in a home that no longer felt like her sanctuary.

Beth took a few hesitant steps across the wine-red carpet. Her pulse throbbed nervously beneath the wound at her scalp.

Kevin Grove shifted on his feet. His mouth thinned into a grim line.

Beth tucked a wisp of hair behind her ear and felt the nubby knit of the black cap she still wore. Oh.

"I suppose you want your cap—"

"I didn't find any other signs of—"

They blurted their words together, fell silent and waited for the other to speak.

"Keep the hat," he finally said.

He probably wouldn't want it back with her blood staining the lining of it anyway. Beth moved another step closer, pulling the sweater she'd changed into more tightly around her middle. "I was wondering if you'd found any answers since you've been here. Was he after my things? Or *me*."

"You've got good locks on your windows, all the doors are sealed tight."

"That's not an answer."

His long coat drifted back around him as he reached up and scrubbed his fingers across the stubble on his jaw. The weary sigh that lifted his shoulders belied the piercing intensity of his eyes. "I can't promise he won't be back to finish whatever he started."

"I know. You won't promise anything you don't know to be a fact." Her effort to force a smile fell short. "Have I mentioned how lousy you are in the public relations department?"

"More than once. Here." He dug into the deep pocket of his tan coat and pulled out her cell phone. "It's a little worse for wear, but it still works."

"You found it."

"Underneath your lawnmower." His long stride matched two of hers as he met her halfway and laid the scratched-up phone in her hand. Beth squeezed it tight. A little normalcy had just returned to her life. Comfort and self-assurance should follow soon enough. She hoped.

"And take this." He pulled a business card from the leather wallet behind his badge, and slipped that into her hand, as well. "It has the precinct number as well as my cell. If you remember anything else, if you find something *is* missing, you can call."

Tipping her chin up to hold his gaze, Beth hugged the card and phone to her chest. She wasn't too tired to smile after all. "I promise I won't bother you in the middle of the night again."

He dipped his head a fraction, shrinking the distance between them. "'Bother' me if you come home late again and sense that something here isn't right. If I don't hear you, Daisy will."

"You want me to rouse Daisy the thunder dog again? Won't she try to eat me?"

"Trust me. She's part mastiff, part pit bull and part couch potato. Not anywhere as mean as she looks or sounds."

Beth's eyes fixed on that whiskey-brown gaze, looking beyond the angles and rough masculinity of his face. Were there any similarities between the dog and her owner? There was nothing soft or safe-looking about Kevin Grove. And yet, despite insult and inconvenience, he'd gone out of his way to take care of her tonight. How wrong would it be for her to take that last frightened step and burrow into the warmth emanating from his chest? How strange was it for her to want that intimate connection with her gruff, sarcastic, make-no-bones-about-anything neighbor?

"You were my knight in shining armor tonight, Kevin."

"No, I wasn't," he corrected. He straightened, his warm eyes chilling as if she'd uttered a curse. "I'm just a cop doing my job."

He'd been more than that. More than a medic, more than a police officer taking down her report. Was being nice evidence of weakness to him? Did he think his kindnesses to her might dilute his tough-guy image?

As if.

"Well, Mr. Cop…I'm going to thank you anyway. For everything." Beth held out her hand. He stared down at the brave appendage, as if he couldn't quite remember what the gesture of friendship meant. Or didn't trust it. Beth waited, hand outstretched. "Don't be rude."

He blinked and angled his gaze back to hers, a trace of amusement shading the amber depths. "There's no audience."

"No, there's not." She wiggled her fingers to show she wasn't retreating. "I'm not on the verge of falling down or passing out either. Take it."

"Now who's bossy?"

"Please."

After a momentary hesitation when she thought he might just be callous enough to turn and walk away, he slowly folded his hand around hers. Kevin's palm was broad and warm, his fingers slightly ticklish as they slid over her skin to secure his grip. Beth silently caught her breath at the unexpected assault on her senses. Her sensitive fingertips brushed across the nearly invisible golden hairs on the back of his hand and prickled at the contact. The size and strength of his hand surrounding hers was no surprise. But the suppleness of movement, the gentleness of his touch, sent ribbons of heat up her arm that spread through her body and warmed her deep inside.

The two of them didn't shake hands so much as they stood there at arm's length, eyes locked—squeezing their fingers lightly around each other's grip, memorizing the other person's touch, absorbing heat.

"He won't be back to finish anything tonight, Beth." Kevin's hushed, articulate tone quickened the fire flowing through her veins. "I promise you that."

"I believe you." With eyes that serious and a voice that sure, how could she not?

Holding on to Kevin Grove was weird. Wonderful. But his sharing anything more than professional concern was probably a complete manufacture of her frightened, weary imagination.

Having made her point about manners and gratitude, Beth pulled away before her unplanned attraction to the cop next door evolved into something that could embarrass one or both of them. "You know, among civilized people, the standard reply when someone says 'Thank you' is 'You're welcome.'"

The sardonic arch of his brow made her question the sincerity of his answering smile. "Lock the dead bolt behind me."

She didn't really think she was going to tame her beastly neighbor with a single handshake and a smile, did she?

Without so much as a "Good night" or "See you later," he pulled on a pair of black leather gloves and stepped outside. He waited on the porch until she'd locked the door knob and slid the dead bolt into place. Beth peeked through the side window to see him pause on the top step and turn up the collar of his coat. He still wore that bulldog-ish grin when he glanced back over his shoulder. After a curt nod, Kevin Grove moved beyond the light from her porch and plunged into the snow.

Once he hit his own front steps, Beth turned off the porch light and rested her forehead against the doorframe. "You're not as scary as you look, detective."

But the charged warmth of her interactions with Kevin Grove quickly dissipated, leaving Beth almost too exhausted to stand. With the end-of-the-year board meeting looming on the horizon, Dr. Landon would need her at work tomorrow—accident or no. Besides, she didn't want to spend any more time than she had to at home until she could shake the irrational fear that some stranger was still lurking about the place, watching her.

She'd better try to get a few hours' sleep.

With the doors all locked up tight, Beth managed to drag her feet down the hallway to get into her pajamas. When she went to brush her teeth, she got her first good look at her pale reflection in the mirror.

"Yikes." No wonder Dr. Rodriguez-Grant had suspected some kind of abuse.

Pulling off the black KCPD watch cap, she turned her head to get a better look at the blue-violet welt on her cheekbone. The white rectangle of gauze and tape covered the stitches along her hairline and most of the dark brown hair at her temple. If it weren't for her bangs and the bruise and those pesky freckles across her cheeks, she'd have no color at all on her face. Instead of a strong, twenty-five-year-old career woman, she looked like some kind of unfortunate waif.

And she'd thought Kevin Grove's appearance was shocking. With a humorless laugh, she pulled the cap back on, savoring its toasty warmth. She must have taken a pretty good blow to the head to think that there was some sort of chemistry between them. He really was just a cop doing his job.

And she was a woman who really needed to get some sleep so she could do her own work in a few hours. She'd been damn lucky to get the position at GlennCo. Her title might be executive assistant now, but Charles Landon had also recommended her for the pharmaceutical giant's executive development program. She was already working behind the scenes with the highest echelon of company leaders. By the time she learned all they had to teach her, she'd be finished with the formal training program. In two years' time—three, tops— she'd be hiring her own assistant for the office *she* was in charge of.

As long as she didn't let anything like an attack in her own home, a puzzling new neighbor or lack of sleep derail her.

Fighting off the fatigue for a few minutes longer, Beth put her computer back together and sat down in the mess of her home office to log on and send an e-mail to her boss. With her apologies, she told Dr. Landon that she'd had an "accident", a late night at the E.R., and that she wouldn't be in until noon.

After logging off, she dragged herself across the hall, set her cell phone beside the business card on her bedside table, and finally crawled into bed, pulling the quilts up to her chin. She closed her eyes and lay there for a few minutes—breathing deeply, picturing images of all the positives in her life, willing herself to relax. She had a healthy family back in central Missouri, a fast track to career success and fuzzy socks to keep her feet warm under the covers. Her Christmas shopping was nearly done. She wanted to go down to the Plaza to pick up some stocking stuffers and a special book for her nephew. But she'd enjoy that—seeing all the Christmas lights and storefront window displays. The stores and restaurants would be open late this time of year—she could even relax with a mug of gourmet hot chocolate. She was going to be all right.

And then she heard it.

Beth's eyes popped open.

Any pretense of serenity ended with the scratchy tap of something against the house outside. She sat up in bed and turned on the lamp. Was there someone in her backyard again? A man running his fingers along the siding and window sills, looking for a way to get in?

It took a few seconds more for her rational mind to convince her racing heart that the sound was nothing more sinister than the wind whipping the plastic tarp Officer Taylor had tacked over her French doors to help keep the heat inside her house.

"He won't be back to finish anything tonight, Beth."

Beth glanced at the curtains, imagining the darkness outside her bedroom window, the white bungalow just beyond and the man inside. She wished Kevin Grove's promise was as easy to believe now that she was all alone as it had been when he'd been holding her hand.

After tuning her radio to a country music station to drown out the wind and her imagination, Beth tucked the KCPD card and her cell phone beneath her pillow. The faintest of electronic feedback noise whirred through the background of the first two cowboy tunes, grinding at her peace of mind like some kind of subliminal taunt.

"I believe you," she whispered, reaching back to shut off the disquieting music. The danger was over. She'd be all right.

Instead of stretching up to turn off the lamp, as well, she rolled onto her side. She pulled the extra pillow against her stomach and curled up into a ball around it, pretending sleep would come as easily tonight as it had every other night of her life.

SHE WAS SLEEPING with the lights on.

Kevin sat in the darkness of his upstairs

bedroom, absently stroking the patchy fur of the big dog snoring on the bed beside him. Daisy's brindle hide was surprisingly smooth, despite the bald patches where medicine and the dedicated staff at the rescue shelter clinic had finally healed her skin. But it was nowhere near as soft or cool to the touch as Beth Rogers's skin had been.

What had that been about in her living room tonight? Bantering clever words? Making promises? Touching her?

If Sheila Mercer hadn't opened his eyes to just how stupid it was for him to care about someone, would he have tugged on Beth's hand and pulled her into his arms? He'd wanted to. She wasn't part of the plan he'd made for his life, wasn't a case he'd been assigned to, wasn't someone he should be worried about even now—yet every male cell in him had wanted to wrap his body around hers and chase the fear from those muted blue eyes.

He had his own investigations to deal with, notes he should be reviewing before the morning's shift briefing. It wasn't his place to watch her house from his bedroom window, to make sure the shadows moving in the night could all be identified and dismissed. He watched a Christmas banner, caught by the wind, tumble through her backyard to tangle in his fence. A rabbit scurried from one hidey-hole to the next. But nothing human. Nothing dangerous.

Traitorous hormones weren't the only thing keeping him awake at 5:42 a.m., however.

There was something about that whole crime scene that nagged at him—something he couldn't yet put his finger on. While simply beating up a woman for the hell of it wasn't unheard of in his line of work, fifteen years of investigative experience told him there had to be a reason either for the break-in or the attack. But there'd been no evidence for either. What did a twenty-five-year-old country girl in the big city possess that was worth the risk of accidentally killing her? Why throw such a scare into her? Who in her life might want to hurt her?

Or was he falling into the same trap all over again—seeing a threat where none existed? Getting involved despite knowing what a lie and a pretty face could cost him?

Daisy grumbled in her sleep and stretched out, pushing her weight against Kevin's leg.

He pulled his fingers from her fur and let at least one of them relax.

"We're two of a kind, aren't we, Daisy girl?" Kevin peeled off the sweater he still wore and tossed it into the darkness beyond the foot of the bed. He pulled the chain from around his neck and placed his badge next to the holstered Glock on his nightstand. "Big, ugly sons of guns with no sense of who or what we should care about."

Daisy's former owner had chained her in the back-yard and left her to starve and become riddled with a skin disease. Kevin had trusted his heart to a woman who'd seen him as an easy mark. By the time Sheila was done laughing at his declaration of love, jeopardizing his career at KCPD and suing him for harassment to cover her own misdeeds, Kevin had been ready to withdraw from all but his closest friends—and to write off pretty women who showed any interest in him entirely.

Yet here he was, keeping a lonely vigil over Beth Rogers.

Logic and experience told him to assign watchdog duty to someone else. It was the curse of his conscience that he couldn't.

THE RECTANGULAR LAMP at the center of the table provided the only light in the luxuriously appointed room.

Some of the people here probably thought the lights were low to hide their gathering in the building at this time of night when most good folks were sleeping. Or that shadowed eyes and veiled faces made confrontation easier. One fool might think it was a kindness to hide the angry faces all eager to lash out at him.

He dimmed the lights because he wanted to. And these people needed to understand that what *he* wanted was more important than anyone else's concerns. It was a subtle, yet effective, reminder that not only was he in charge here, but he was taking control of this untenable situation that had been thrust upon them.

The dark figure pacing in front of the floor-to-ceiling windows was painfully aware of that fact. That's why the meeting had been called, why he was pleading his case. "I'm an old man feeling my mortality, that's all. I had an attack of conscience. Our research proves the drug is too risky. I had no idea the repercussions would be so…personal…for all of us."

"So you're saying you're not behind the letters we all received?"

"No." The old man opened up his briefcase and tossed a similarly addressed plain white envelope—no stamp, no postmark, no fingerprints or DNA to trace—on the table. "I got one, too. The demands are the same, I'm sure. We're all being blackmailed."

"No one is taking this company away from us. The drug works," the man at the head of the table reminded him. "This shouldn't even be an issue."

"Yes, the drug works initially. But at what cost? I know you altered the results of the clinical trials so you could move it into production next year, despite my recommendation that the lab needed more time."

The man at the head of the table savored a long swallow from his old-fashioned glass before patting his jacket and the unsigned letter he'd tucked into the breast pocket underneath. The ten-million-dollar demand wouldn't bankrupt him, but if they couldn't find their blackmailer and eliminate the problem, the threat of more and more demands eventually would.

Even if he wasn't behind this scheme to

extort money from each of them, the old man had set the wheels in motion with a very costly mistake of conscience. "And I know you made more than one copy of the original test results."

The gray-haired man's face blanched a deathly white. Ironic. Or perhaps a mere foreshadowing of events to come? "I'm a medical scientist. Of course, I'd keep all the research the lab produces."

"And you didn't think there'd be a problem with two sets of documentation?"

The old man had some fight in him yet. "Your greed is what created the problem. I just wanted to delay the project. Give my staff more time. With another year, maybe two, we could adjust the formula to reduce the side effects. My caution now could save us millions in lawsuits later."

"We needed to move forward instead of dragging our feet." He took another drink, letting the aged bourbon burn through his anger. "A two-month delay could cost us a rather generous paycheck. Two *years?* We'd be out of business."

The woman to his left smacked her palm atop the table, demanding to be heard. "But someone out there still knows. Did you think about anybody else when you had this attack of conscience? Forget the money. We could go to jail if this gets out. For a very long time."

A large man unfolded from the shadows and planted himself in front of the man who was pacing. "I should throw you out that window right now for being so reckless. An attack of conscience…" he muttered. "The people in this room *were* the only ones who know about that project. Now you've let the cat out of the bag and we're paying for it."

"At least I discovered the problem so we could do something about it before the authorities pick up our trail and shut us down. If it was left up to you, we never would have found out."

There *was* that. The man running this clandestine meeting set his drink on the table with a deliberate crack of glass against wood, commanding the large man's attention. He'd already handled one discreet job for him earlier tonight. "Are you prepared to do what needs to be done?"

"Give me the order." My, he was eager to please.

The pacing man protested. "*I'll* handle it."

"How can I trust you? You made copies of incriminating evidence." He traced his finger around the rim of the glass and touched the last drop of whiskey to his tongue, savoring the burning sensation. "I can do damage control. But I can't handle a traitor in my midst."

"Traitor? How could I? I'm in this, too. It was a stupid mistake. I see that now."

"So you'll help us cover our trail?"

Good God, the wind chill was below zero outside, and his old friend was sweating as he nodded agreement. "Give me one more chance. I'll make this right."

He surveyed the room for a consensus of shrugs and nods before making his own decision. "Very well. One more chance. But remember…there's not one of us willing to pay for your failure."

"I understand."

"As long as we're all clear on this. You make this go away." He stood, buttoning his blazer as he looked down at the man who had every reason to be worried. "Or we will."

Chapter Four

"Anything else for the good of the cause today?" KCPD's Fourth Precinct Chief Mitch Taylor pulled off his reading glasses and set them on the podium at the front of the third-floor conference room. "Yeah, Banning?"

As he took a question from a table in the back, Kevin unzipped his work folder and tucked his copy of the morning briefing agenda inside. It was a typical Tuesday morning at Fourth Precinct headquarters—check in, grab coffee, wake up, eavesdrop on the latest gossip, sit down and listen to an overview of KCPD's open cases and potential concerns around the Kansas City metro area. While different detectives took charge of different investigations, and uniforms patrolled the streets, it didn't hurt to have all eyes open for a lead that might pop on someone else's case. The morning briefing was about teamwork and focus…and grabbing a spare minute to scan the background check he'd run on Beth Rogers.

He flipped to the next page in his folder and read the brief report. Driver's license. Car registration. Never married. Squeaky clean except for one parking ticket. Nothing before last night's incident filed by her or against her.

As conversations broke out across the room, signaling the meeting was drawing to a close, Kevin turned to the next page, listing 9-1-1 calls to their street in the past few months. Two ambulance calls to one of those elderly neighbors Beth had mentioned. The only criminal complaint was a misdemeanor noise violation against her good buddy, Hank Whitaker—revving up his snowblower late at night while children were trying to sleep. He hadn't responded to the neighbor's phone call. Probably hadn't heard anything at all if Beth's description of the man was accurate.

Whatever had happened last night, it wasn't about the humdrum suburban neighborhood. *He* was probably the scariest thing on the block.

When his new partner, Atticus Kincaid, pushed back his chair beside him, Kevin knew the meeting was over. He closed his folder, respectfully turning his attention to one of the few men in the room who could match him for size and stature.

Chief Taylor wrapped it up. "I shouldn't have to remind you that the weatherman is predicting more snow this afternoon and into the evening. And 'tis the season for stress—only ten shopping days until Christmas." That earned a few laughs and groans from the room. "Traffic and tempers could both be a little dicey today. Watch your backs out there. Dismissed."

"Yo, amigo." A. J. Rodriguez pulled away from the line of officers filing out of the room and sat on the front edge of the long table, crossing his arms over the shoulder holster he wore. A veteran detective like Kevin, he now spent a good deal of his time training and handling younger undercover officers. "I hear you were up late with my sister last night."

The expected hoots and ribald comments from the men and women within earshot bounced off Kevin's hide. Without missing a beat, he stood, towering over A.J. "She couldn't wait to check me out, huh?"

"Called me first thing this morning. Emilia was worried about her patient—said she showed signs of a deliberate attack and suspected abuse." A.J. was a hard man to read, but Kevin couldn't sense any accusation in his mildly accented tone. "I said the bulldog was a good guy."

"Thanks."

A.J. rose as his partner, tall, blond Josh Taylor—the chief's cousin—joined them with a typically wiseass grin. Now *this* guy could do some teasing. "I'm more interested in hearing about that sweet brunette. My nephew, Alex, said that minus the bruises and bandages, she's a hottie. And probably damn lucky that you were there to help her."

"There's nothing to tell." Kevin straightened his tie, collected his mug of coffee and notebook and turned to leave. "Elisabeth Rogers lives next door to me. She was… injured in her home last night. I drove her to the E.R. End of story."

"So you didn't notice the big blue eyes and all the curves?"

Alex Taylor had?

A wildly inappropriate and alarmingly intense spike of protective jealousy almost made it to the tip of Kevin's tongue. He channeled the raw emotion into a tight fist at his side. Beth Rogers wasn't his. The Taylors were good people. Young, studly Alex Taylor was much more her type than he'd ever be. "She's pretty."

"And?"

"And nothing." End of discussion.

"Well, that sucks for a happy ending," Josh whined. "What's a man got to do to get a story out of you? Did you talk? Ask her out?"

"I'm not here to entertain you, Taylor. You can do that all by yourself." Kevin's deadpan reply earned a round of laughs. By silent agreement, all four men joined the exodus out of the morning briefing and headed to their respective desks on the main floor.

While Kevin opened his folder and pulled some crime-scene photos from a lab report to add to his notes, Atticus settled in at the desk facing him. His partner sorted through a stack of phone messages, tossed them aside, then braced his elbows on the desktop and leaned forward. "So what's the real scoop between you and the 'sweet brunette'?" he pressed. "There's more going on than what you told Josh and A.J."

"What, like a relationship? I just met her."

"Something happened. Did she turn you down?"

"I didn't ask."

Atticus's pause lasted long enough that Kevin stopped his work and looked up. "But you do want to ask her out."

Kevin shook his head, pretending those laser-sharp eyes weren't seeing right through him. "I work with your family on one murder investigation, and suddenly you think you know me?"

"That murder was my father," Atticus countered, not fooled for an instant. "My brothers and I owe you big time for seeing it through to the end and arresting his killer. You even took a bullet for us in the process. I think that qualifies you as family. So, as an adopted member of the Kincaid clan, I'm allowed to pester you on this."

"That's your logic?"

"Flawless, isn't it?" Kevin went back to work. Atticus let the subject rest for all of two seconds. "Now tell me about the 'hottie.' You said you'd sworn off women after the harassment investigation."

"I was just helping the lady out. She'd sustained a concussion and had no business driving."

"Right." Atticus nodded toward the notebook on Kevin's desk. "So why did you run a background check on her?"

"You don't miss a trick, do you?"

"My wife taught me an invaluable lesson about paying attention to details."

"What's it been now, six months?" Atticus had married Chief Taylor's assistant, Brooke Hansford, after his father's murder had brought them together. "How's married life treating you?"

"Beautifully," he stated, smiling at the wedding photo displayed proudly on his desk. "Brooke makes me feel like a very smart man for falling in love with her. But you're changing the subject. What's up with—" he rose slightly from his chair to read the name on the top of Kevin's papers "—Elisabeth Rogers? She's not on our case list, yet you're investigating her."

There was no arguing with the brains of this operation. Leaning forward, he mirrored

Atticus's position. "All right, so I'm a little concerned. Beth wasn't injured in an accident. She was attacked, her home broken into. But I've got no motive—and no idea if the perp will try to hurt her again."

Elisabeth had become *Beth*. Kevin's tone grew hushed. Inside, he braced and waited. But Atticus could be counted on to be discreet if things sounded more personal than they should have.

"You heard the chief—the crazies are out this time of year." Atticus threw out ideas the way they would with any of the crimes they dealt with. "What's her family like? Could someone have an issue with them that they're taking out on her?"

"They're from a farm outside a small town in central Missouri. No K.C. connection I know of."

"Risky behaviors?"

"I asked. Nothing. As far as I can tell, she works and…" What else? He'd seen paint cans in the spare bedroom, a basket of knitting on the sofa and plenty of papers, books and computer disks in her home office. "…works some more."

With a sage nod, Atticus sat back in his chair.

"Why don't you start there? Could be something going on at her job. What does she do?"

Kevin read from the notes he'd jotted in the early hours when he hadn't been sleeping this morning. "Executive assistant at GlennCo Pharmaceuticals. Works for the chief of the research and product development division."

"I saw in the business pages that Raymond Glenn and most of his board of directors made the Forbes 500 list. Even in this economy, their business is thriving. What kind of money does she make?"

Shaking his head, Kevin closed the notebook. "It wasn't a robbery. She's as middle class as we are. Just bought her first house. Doesn't have enough furniture to fill all the rooms yet. It was probably a random crazy like you said."

"Uh-huh." Atticus wasn't buying the *whatever* tone in Kevin's voice. "We don't call you the bulldog around here because of your good looks. You'll be checking out GlennCo the minute we break for lunch."

Kevin accepted the compliment as he was meant to, then got up to retrieve his coat from the back of his chair. "Yeah, but that's just because you leave me alone every day for your standing lunch date with Brooke. I have to do something to keep myself out of trouble."

"Seriously, if there's anything I can do, let me know. Like I said, the Kincaids owe you. On the clock or off, just ask." Atticus stood and put on his coat, as well. "In the meantime, we've got the murder of a homeless man up by the river we need to get on before the weather hits. Ready to go to work?"

Time to set aside his fixation with the wounded beauty who'd pounded her way into his isolated life. Kevin pulled his badge from beneath his tie and let it hang squarely down the front of his open coat. "It's what I do best."

"YES, MR. GLENN. I'll give him the message as soon as he's available." Elisabeth jotted down the reminder from Raymond Glenn, the company's CEO. "I'll make sure Dr. Landon copies you on tomorrow's presentation before the board meeting."

"Good." He thanked her before ending the phone call. "I'll see you at the meeting tomorrow, then. Have a good day."

"Thank you, sir…" But he'd already disconnected the call.

Elisabeth hung up the phone at her desk and glanced over her shoulder at the adjoining office door behind her. No rest for the weary, beat-up, missed-a-morning-at-work assistant like her. It was time.

She waited until the strains of classical music behind the door ended before she lightly knocked on her boss's door. "It's one o'clock, Dr. Landon."

A giggle and a scuffle from the other side made her smile and politely bide her time before entering. Charles Landon was a fit, handsome, seventy-year-old man who'd continued to work after retirement age because he still had ideas about healing people, and skills to teach her and the other young pups at GlennCo Pharmaceuticals about turning a dream into a thriving business empire.

His early-morning trysts and lunchtime rendezvous with his fourth wife might not be the most professional of behavior, but he always scheduled their "meetings" before work hours or over meal breaks. And more often than not, he and his wife would come and go via the private elevator in his office, avoiding embarrassing Beth or anyone else with their clandestine get-togethers. If a busy man as hard-working and well respected as Charles Landon wanted to steal an hour here and there to get busy with his wife, then he deserved a little privacy and discretion from the woman who ran his office.

And Beth had quickly learned that that loyalty went both ways. When the board had argued about her boss hiring someone from outside the company—a woman as young as she was—he'd gone to bat for her, claiming fresh ideas and youthful energy were what had propelled him and his partners to success, and that it was a smart go-getter like Beth who would maintain the company's success.

She knocked again. "Dr. Landon?"

She heard the scrape of a lock disengaging and the door connecting the suite of offices swung open.

"My, God, Elisabeth—look at you." Charles Landon had his hand on Beth's back and was guiding her to the leather settee in his office before she even had a chance to hand him his messages. "Please, my dear. Sit."

Beth cleared her throat, slyly pointing to the smudge of red lipstick on Charles's mouth.

"Oh." He pulled out a handkerchief and wiped his lips. "Sorry."

Deborah Landon was pinning her long, curly blond hair into place as she sat beside Beth. "What happened? Did you have an accident? The roads are so treacherous this time of year."

"No."

Charles slipped his hands over his wife's shoulders and pulled her back to her feet. His face was flushed as he guided her to the rolling chair behind his desk and the fur coat draped over it. "I'm sorry to chase you away so soon, dear. But I'd better take a look at Elisabeth's injuries and make sure she's all right."

"Charles, I'm fine," Beth insisted. "Ready to go to work if you are."

Deborah giggled at the protest. "Charlie's feeling a little guilty right now, hon. Let him fuss over you." She tapped her husband's lips with a bright red nail before giving him a kiss and a smile. "It's what he does best." She wriggled her fingers to make sure Beth noticed the large, yellow diamond ring she sported on her right hand. "Early Christmas present. Sometimes I think buying me goodies is the only way he can tell me how much he loves me."

"Deborah," he cautioned, smiling back. "I told you I was sorry I've had to work so many hours lately. It's the end of the year—you know how that goes."

"He hasn't even taken time off to do any Christmas shopping." Deborah straightened Charles's tie and smoothed his collar and jacket. "I don't know your grandchildren the way you do. How can I be sure they'll like what I picked out for them?"

"I know they'll love them. You'd better go, dear. I promise to take a look at those gifts tonight. Thanks for helping out." Beth turned her face to the windows as husband and wife shared another kiss. "And thanks for stopping by."

"You know I always enjoy when we can spend a little time together, sweetie. Elisabeth? Make sure he takes his pills."

Summoned to join the conversation once more, Beth nodded. Heart medication was a serious thing. "I will."

Charles walked Deborah to the back of his office and opened a closet door. Inside, he pressed a button to open the waiting elevator door. "Now who's fussing over whom?"

"I didn't say you were the only one who was good at it." Deborah looked over his shoulder to say goodbye to Beth. "Make sure he doesn't forget to do a little more Christmas shopping for me, too."

"I'll remind him," Beth grinned. "Gucci purse, right?"

"She's a keeper, Charlie. I'll see you at home."

Charles and Deborah traded waves and kisses as the elevator door closed. Then, with a resolute sigh, Charles shut the closet door and turned back to Beth at the settee. "Now, young lady. Tell me about last night. Were you mugged? I kept you here too late, didn't I?"

Beth waved aside his concern and offered up an appreciative smile. "It's not as bad as it looks."

"It looks as if it hurts like hell." His eyes narrowed with fatherly concern. "Tonight I'm having security walk you to your car. I'll have them follow you all the way home."

"No, you won't."

"You should have taken the whole day

off." She could tell by the fussy movements of his hands on his clothes and thinning hair that he wanted to do something for her—make something right.

But he wasn't her father, and she wasn't about to become a basket case because some nut job had gotten into her house. Despite how inviting a long nap and some TLC sounded right about now, she knew it was important to keep moving. Sitting still allowed time for shadowy figures and unexplained noises to creep into her mind and resurrect the isolated helplessness that had plagued what few dreams she'd had last night.

"According to my list, we have a lot to do to get ready for tomorrow's board meeting. Mr. Glenn wants a copy of your presentation before the meeting."

"Of course, he does. What else?"

Beth set the folder she carried on the middle of his mahogany desk, and picked up the bottle of pills and glass of water waiting there. While he took his medicine, Beth nodded toward the file. "If you don't sign off on that rough draft of Dr. Allen's clinical trial report by the end of the day, it won't be ready to present to Mrs. Landon for inclusion in the January stockholder's report."

"I wish you'd stop referring to Geneva as 'Mrs. Landon.'" He stuffed the pill bottle into his pocket before crossing to the refreshment bar next to the settee. "I'm married to Deborah now."

"It's awkward to refer to the vice president of Public Relations as 'The First Mrs. Landon.' And because she hasn't invited me to call her by her first name yet…"

"Geneva's an iron butterfly. Too proud of all she had to overcome to be such a success. Too afraid of losing it all to drop her guard for an instant." Charles poured himself a cup of coffee and stirred in two spoonfuls of sugar. Beth declined his offer to pour one for her. "You're smart. You're climbing the corporate ladder, and yet you've remained very much a lady. I'm afraid my first wife has forgotten how to be one."

"Lady, I'm staying."

Lady. Kevin Grove's voice made a distracting, unexpectedly welcome entrance into Beth's thoughts, warming her inside the suit she wore. At one point last night, his use of the term—as if he'd been rudely trying to drive her away by not even acknowledging her name—had finally eroded her patience with him. But by the time he'd made it clear he wasn't going to leave *her* in her time of need, the word had taken on a different meaning.

With the intensity of those whiskey-colored eyes to back up the rich timbre of his voice, *Lady* became a nickname of sorts—a private joke between them. A connection.

It was hard to imagine the brawny, quick-witted detective whispering anything remotely soft or romantic to a woman. But she could well believe that the words he did utter would be unambiguous and full of emotion. If he called her a lady, it was because he saw her that way. Not because he called every female on the planet *honey* or *sweetie* or *dear*.

"Elisabeth, dear…" The scent of dry-cleaned wool told her that Charles had come up behind her.

She blinked away the odd feelings that had lingered since her encounter with Kevin Grove last night. "Yes, sir?"

"I don't want you to overtax yourself this

afternoon. You make me feel guilty for working you so hard." With a firm hand on her shoulder, he guided her into the burgundy leather chair where she normally sat during their meetings. She winced at the pressure on the bruises beneath her navy jacket. "Sorry."

"I'm fine."

Instead of moving on, he set down his cup and pulled over the matching chair to sit close. He squinted as he leaned in to inspect her face. His silvering eyebrows arched with concern. "Is it a sharp, shooting pain or a continuous ache?"

When his long fingers hovered toward her face, Beth raised her hand and blocked him from touching her. Sympathy from the boss wasn't how she wanted to move up the corporate ladder. "If…we could just get our work done. I'd really love to be home early and get a full night's sleep tonight."

"Elisabeth, I *am* a doctor by training. Just because I retired from my practice and went into business—"

"I went to the hospital last night, Dr. Landon. I saw a perfectly kind, extremely thorough emergency-room doctor. She gave me a list of warning signs to watch for, but said that as long as none of them cropped up and I felt fine, that I could work today."

"We're back to 'Dr. Landon,' are we?" The lines on his forehead seemed to be unusually pronounced as he swept his gaze over her face. The taut compression of his mouth seemed to reflect genuine concern. "I suppose that means I've overstepped my bounds again. You know my children are all grown and out of the house. I have to worry about somebody."

"I'm okay," she reiterated. "But I'd consider it a personal favor if you could get me out of here by six tonight."

"Of course, dear." He shook off the troubled thoughts that lined his face and stood, carrying his coffee cup around the desk and taking his spot in his overstuffed leather chair. "Of course." He picked up the rough draft of the report and waved it like a rally flag. "I want to take the very best care of you I can. You keep my secrets. You don't judge me. You've improved the efficiency of this office immeasurably since you started here in August. I'd hate it if I lost you. The company would hate it."

She wasn't so sure if the *company* would

agree with that. But with the width of the desk and the sincerity of his compassion between them, Beth found it easy to match his smile. "It's a bump on the head, Charles. I'm not planning on going anywhere anytime soon."

"Good. Because I am." Pulling his glasses from his inside jacket pocket signaled that he was getting down to work and that she needed to, as well. "Deborah reminded me that I'm an old fart who spends entirely too much time at the office. Some time off would reduce the number of these gray hairs and lower my blood pressure. I'm thinking of surprising her with a weeklong getaway between Christmas and New Year's. Will you check into the availability of a suite at this resort?" He pulled a colorful brochure from the same pocket and handed it across the desk. "We spent our honeymoon in the Caymans. That sounds like a nice Christmas present, yes?"

"It sounds like an expensive one." Beth made the notation on her daily planner. "The airfare alone on this short notice will set you back a pretty penny. I assume you'll want first class?"

"Absolutely. I've gotten my priorities mixed up lately. I want to spend quality time with the people who are most important in my life." His gaze drifted to the corner of his office where the elevator had gone silent, and his voice took on an almost-wistful tone. "No matter what it costs me."

Crazily enough, the sudden mood swing into Shakespearean tragedy sounded sincere. Had she just gotten an explanation for his recent erratic behavior? "Sir? Maybe this is none of my business, but…is everything all right—with you and Deborah?"

He blinked. Focused. "I am married to a beautiful woman who deserves better than a few office visits and phone calls telling her to go on to bed without me because GlennCo needs me to stay late at the office one more time. This is my fourth go at marriage. I think I'd better start getting it right, don't you?"

Marrying a woman closer to his age than her own might help in that regard, too, but Beth kept that opinion to herself. "I think working to make your relationship a success is always an admirable thing, sir." Beth stood and pushed the chair he'd moved back into its place. "I'll find you a lovely spot in the Cayman Islands, I promise."

"Good girl." Running his fingers beneath his collar, he stretched his neck, as though just realizing the hand-tailored cotton had too much starch in it. He repeated the action a second time before opening the report and glancing at the first page. He closed it again just as quickly and looked up. "Elisabeth…have you run across my flash drive containing the research data for the clinical trials of Gehirn 330?"

"The Alzheimer's drug treatment GlennCo is developing?" She shook her head. "I haven't seen anything beyond the preliminary outline for that project. I thought it was still in the experimental phase—that we were tabling its release for another couple of years."

"No. We've moved up the timetable to next summer. I know you sometimes take work home."

"I don't have the security clearance to remove anything that sensitive from the building." Was *this* the reason for his weird behavior? The urgency of finding the missing data could explain a lot. "I saw you put your hard copy and the memory stick in your safe yesterday morning after your meeting with Dr. Shaw from the lab."

"I looked."

"Did you check your briefcase?"

Charles Landon's face blanched to an alarming shade of pale before his cheeks flushed with color. "*You* don't have it?"

She shook her head, wondering if he'd been worrying over the wrong patient. "Why would I?"

He grew more agitated by the second. "It wasn't in the stack of files you were putting away last night?"

"No."

"Could it have fallen into your purse or attaché?"

"Not that I know of." Oh, my God. If it had, after last night the tiny flash drive could have landed anywhere in her car or garage. It could even have been scratched or erased. An inexplicable foreboding quickened her pulse. "I'm certain I haven't seen the Gehirn 330 data since your meeting yesterday."

"You're sure?"

Why was he putting her on the defensive like this? "I'll call Dr. Shaw and order another copy from the lab."

Charles peered over the top of his glasses as if she'd spouted gibberish. "No."

"Should I notify security?"

"No!"

Beth's eyes widened at the sharp reprimand.

Charles was on his feet in an instant, holding his hand up in apology. "I'm sorry, dear. I'm sorry." He tossed his glasses on top of the desk and smoothed his fingers over his hair, breathing deeply to compose himself. "I guess my wife is right. I fuss over things too much."

She accepted his apology, but not the immediate dismissal of his frantic concern. "Is there something on that flash drive or in that report you need for tomorrow's board meeting? Are you worried about industrial espionage? Someone stealing a formula? You haven't been yourself lately. And I don't think it's job stress."

"You have no idea." Charles Landon was a tall, healthy man. He doctored his shortcomings and maintained a cyclist's trim figure to keep up with the wives who were getting younger with each subsequent marriage. But the sigh that sagged his shoulders now left him looking haggard and old. "You

have a good head on your shoulders, Elisabeth. You'll need that."

Cryptic. "For what?"

He sank back down in his chair, his
pensive smile making as little sense as his
outburst over the missing data had. "Just
book me on that flight to the Caymans. I have
a lot of work to do."

"Yes, sir."

Beth watched his graying head bowed over
the report for a few seconds before leaving
his office and softly closing the door behind
her. She set her planner on her desk and
pulled up the number for the travel agent the
company typically used on her phone. But
she stopped short of punching in the number.

Instead, she pulled open the center drawer
of her desk and looked inside, moving aside
pens and paperclips to look beneath them.
Nothing that shouldn't be there.

She opened the top left drawer and moved
the stapler back to the right-hand side where
she liked to keep it. A blip of awareness, of
something not as it should be, stopped her.

She opened the drawer again. When had
she moved her stapler?

With sharper focus, closer study, she

opened the rest of her drawers. Then she pushed back her chair and crossed to the shelves and file cabinets lining the wall on either side of her window. Here and there she found something that was slightly off—a tray of computer disks with the lid down but not latched, the bent tab of a file folder, a pot of English ivy sitting on the edge of its saucer.

The cleaning crew sometimes moved her family pictures and other knickknacks when they dusted. But inside her desk?

Had her boss gone through her office?

She glanced back at Charles Landon's door. Just how important was that missing data? Could his job be at stake? Hers?

Some of that same paranoia from last night crept back to life inside her, drumming beneath the wound at her temple. Did someone think she had that memory stick?

She'd tear her garage apart top to bottom if she had to, pull up the carpet in her Jeep. But no way had that flash drive been on her desk or among her things. She hadn't taken it.

Slipping her hand inside the pocket of her wool slacks, Beth closed her fingers around the business card she carried with her. Kevin

Grove had said to call him if she remembered anything about the attack—or if something bothered her.

This bothered her.

Someone had searched through her things.

"THERE'S NO ID on this vic, either."

Two bodies in one day. Two elderly men dead in the same neighborhood down by the Missouri River docks. This morning's had been discovered in an alley by a homeless woman, this one by a security guard checking vacant properties in the area.

The muscles around Kevin's left shoulder ached—partly because he'd taken a hit man's bullet there last year and today it was a whopping eight degrees outside. In the fourteen months since that compromised safe house shoot-out, he'd learned that cold and the beat-up places inside him didn't always get along. And yeah, it'd been an extra long day, working his second homicide on next to no sleep. But mostly, he was aching inside because both of the victims had been men his grandmother's age. And the thought of some bastard preying on anyone as frail and beautiful and deserving of long life as Grandma Miriam squeezed a vise around his heart.

There was plenty inside of him aching. But not a bit of it showed on the outside. Not when he had a job to do.

Kevin stuck the tip of his pen inside the pocket of the dead man's tattered flannel shirt and raised the flap, just in case he'd missed a clue. But as he'd suspected from the moment he and Atticus had walked into the abandoned riverfront warehouse, this poor old guy was a John Doe. With a grunt of resignation that fogged the air, Kevin tucked the pen back inside the tweed blazer he wore under his coat. Without a name to start from, their investigation had just gotten a lot more complicated.

"How old do you think this one is?" Atticus knelt on the opposite side of the nearly bald man, carefully cataloguing their observations in his notebook. "Late seventies? Eighties? If he didn't have that hole cut in his gut, I'd say he died of old age or exposure." He traced an imaginary circle in the air around the victim. "But the stabbing didn't happen here. There's not enough blood for this to be the primary crime scene."

Kevin pointed to the end of the dead man's grimy parka sleeve. "He's not homeless, either. He's got some meat on his bones and his fingernails are clean. I doubt these clothes are even his."

Atticus closed his notepad and stood. "Christmas crime-scene cover-up. Not the way I'd planned to spend my holidays."

"Him, either." Bracing his hands on his thighs, Kevin rose, as well.

Atticus grinned at the morbid joke before acknowledging the tall brunette woman who ducked beneath the half-open loading dock door and approached their location inside the warehouse. "M.E.'s office is here. Let's back off and let them do the prelim on the body while we scout out the rest of this place. Where do you want to start?"

"How about with my fist rammed down some bastard's throat?" Okay, so a few of those emotions were leaking out. Inhaling a deep breath, Kevin tried to shake off those lingering emotions. "Two elderly vics, both stabbed to the point of mutilation, no blood at either crime scene. You thinking what I'm thinking?"

Atticus nodded. "These are dump sites.

And I'll hazard a guess that the two deaths are related."

"I wouldn't bet against it."

"Do we have a serial killer?"

A female voice joined the discussion. "More like a cover-up for a botched surgery." Dr. Holly Masterson-Kincaid, the wife of Atticus's oldest brother and the crime lab's chief medical examiner, set her kit down with a weary sigh. "You two do realize that some of us would like to have a few days off around the holidays, right?" She smiled at Atticus and winked a greeting to Kevin. "You boys need to stop finding dead bodies for me."

Atticus raised his hands in mock surrender. "Hey, you're not the only newlywed in the family. The sooner we find answers, the sooner we can all get home to the people we care about."

Yeah. Kevin would get right on that. With Miriam in a nursing home and Sheila thankfully out of his life, it looked like it would be Daisy and him and a big empty house for Christmas morning. Maybe he'd get Daisy to give him a kiss on New Year's Eve.

Of course, peachy lips with a touch of sass

in them sounded much more appealing than a big black nose and dog slobber.

Hell. Where had that thought come from? Kissing Beth Rogers wasn't gonna happen. Not in any reality he needed to be a part of. He shouldn't have carried her in his arms, shouldn't have memorized her sweet and spicy scent—shouldn't have watched over her house or worried about why someone would want to hurt her. Every memory of freckles and pale skin stimulated something in him that was more man than cop.

He'd be wiser to concentrate on the dead bodies than dwell on his lingering fascination with the girl next door.

"So you finished the autopsy from this morning's vic?" he asked, bringing an awkwardly abrupt end to Atticus and Holly's conversation regarding the Kincaid family's holiday plans.

"Yes."

He didn't miss the subtle signal from Atticus to Holly that she should just ignore his partner's Scrooge-ish mood and give them her report.

"Your John Doe from this morning had his liver surgically removed. Post mortem. I believe the other stab wounds were meant to mask the incision." She knelt down beside the corpse on the warehouse floor and pulled his clothing aside. "This one has the same injuries. I won't know for sure until I compare tool marks, but I'd say your two vics were dispatched by the same perp."

"The M.O.s match," Atticus agreed.

"You harvest an organ to sell it on the black market." As she covered up the body, Kevin worked the possible scenarios through his head. "Or to remove evidence of some kind from the body."

Holly rose to stand between them. "Or to cover mistakes by someone who shouldn't be practicing medicine anymore." She squeezed Atticus's arm, and winked up at Kevin. "Why don't you two go do your hunt and search thing while I take care of the body? I'll get us out of here as soon as I can."

Kevin nodded in agreement. "I need some fresh air. I'll check outside—see if I can spot anything to indicate who might have dumped him here."

"I'll start canvassing the neighborhood," Atticus volunteered. "Maybe we'll luck out and find somebody who saw something."

Kevin wasn't holding his breath. Swapping out his plastic gloves for wool-lined leather ones, he turned up his collar against the stiff breeze off the ice-chunked river and went outside to begin a systematic search.

Like the alley this morning, there wasn't much to find. He had a crime-scene investigator photograph some tire marks in the snow drifted against the base of the loading dock, but enough new snow had fallen to make casting them impossible. The CSI scooped up a sample of an oil leak in the same location to take back to the lab for analysis. But there was no blood, no footprints, no sign of a struggle. And it was too cold for potential witnesses to be lurking about.

He hadn't found any answers for Beth Rogers at lunch, and he wasn't finding any answers now. This was turning out to be one hell of a productive day.

Kevin was sitting inside the cab of his SUV, running the heater and thawing out when his cell phone buzzed. Night had fallen, shrinking the world outside to the distance of his headlights—but not so small that the outside world couldn't find him.

Muttering half a curse, he pulled the

phone from his belt. This had better not be another body. Chief Taylor had warned that this was a stressful time of year for some people, but come on.

He read the number. *Unnamed.* At least he could rule out the dispatcher's call to another crime scene. That knowledge didn't necessarily improve his frustrated mood.

He opened the phone. "Yeah?"

A beat of silence, a whisper of breathing.

"Kevin?" His entire world changed with that one word. The breath rushed out of his chest, leaving a rare tranquility in its wake. And, hang it all, he was dangerously close to smiling. "I mean, Detective Grove?"

He liked *Kevin* better.

"Beth?" Any sense of calm was fleeting. Other instinctive reactions took over. There was an out-of-breath quality to her hushed tone. And the way she cleared her throat to mask the catch of emotion made his own voice grow husky. Every wishful, aching cell in his body went on instant alert. "Why are you whispering?"

"I think…"

Were they going to play this game again? So he might not be the easiest person in the world to talk to—just answer the damn question before he got really worried. "You think what?"

"I think someone's following me."

Chapter Five

She was an idiot. A full-blown, bona fide idiot.

Beth cradled the hot chocolate between her hands, wishing she could blame the steaming concoction for the heat that suddenly flooded her cheeks. She peeked over the rim of her plastic cup and watched two small children launch themselves into the arms of the man who'd been staring at her across the bookstore's second-floor cafe.

Not a stalker. Not her attacker. Just somebody's dad who happened to be built like a linebacker.

She took a drink of the hot chocolate, hoping the sugar and caramel and cream would jump-start her sleep-deprived, para-noid brain.

Who wouldn't stare at a woman with a

purple cheekbone and a gauze bandage covering the side of her head? The young father had probably been wondering what size of truck had hit her. Or maybe he was embarrassed that Beth had bumped into him browsing the romance section of the store. He'd seemed so out of place that she'd been suspicious of his presence among the love stories. The sensation of being overrun by a man of considerable size and strength was still fresh enough in her mind that she'd panicked.

He'd come inside the busy store just after she had, hadn't he? Followed her up the escalator? Just happened to turn into the same section of books? With some nefarious purpose in mind, he had to be following her, right? Sheesh.

A woman who must be his wife pushed a stroller up with a third child, greeted him and leaned down to exchange a kiss. As the man stashed the romance novel he'd selected beneath his coat next to him on the bench seat, the heat in Beth's cheeks intensified.

Idiot. This time of year? Thousands of shoppers enjoying the lights and stores on the Plaza? He'd been buying a gift for his wife.

Beth turned away from the lively family tableau and drank the rest of her cocoa. Even though embarrassment rendered the sweet froth nearly tasteless, she needed the warmth of it to fortify her before she picked up her phone and placed a second call to Detective Grove. She wouldn't mind trading more quips with her villainous-looking neighbor, but Beth knew the polite thing was to call him back before he drove all the way through downtown K.C. on a false alarm.

Voice mail. It almost saddened her to think she wouldn't be hearing that deep, masculine voice again. She imagined he'd have something to say about wasting his valuable time. Still, in the name of good neighborly relations, she had to try. Once his message ended, she left her own.

"Hey, detective. Elisabeth Rogers again. It's just after seven. I hope you hear this before you get to the Plaza. I realize we live in the opposite direction, and I'm trying to catch you to tell you to head on home. I'll be going that way myself as soon as I pick up my car from the 47th Street parking garage. At any rate, I'm fine. Just got spooked by my imagination. The man wasn't following me.

Sorry to trouble you." Her breath stuttered out on a self-deprecating sigh. "It was nothing."

With the message sent, Beth bundled up in her bright blue parka, cleared her table and headed downstairs to make her purchases. She'd already dropped off her long brown dress coat at the cleaner's to get the blood out of the wool, and had planned to stop at a railroad hobbyist shop to get a gift for her father. But now she figured the smart plan was to simply climb into her Jeep, go home and get to bed. Once these last 24 hours were behind her, her life would probably go back to being unremarkably normal again.

And Kevin Grove would go back to being the mysterious monster of a man next door.

The cold outside cleared Beth's head of odd longings and paranoia more effectively than any amount of rational thinking had. "Brr."

With two books and a holiday-themed jigsaw puzzle weighing down a bag on one side, Beth switched her leather purse to her right arm, sliding it high onto her shoulder and tucking it securely against her side. Icy crystals of snow nipped her face as she waited for a break in traffic to dash across to the median and then on to the sidewalk on the opposite side of the street.

The J. C. Nichols Plaza, with more than a million Christmas lights lining every rooftop, arch and tower throughout the holiday season, glowed with an air of frosted twilight. Despite the wet weather, the sidewalks were full of shoppers and tourists and those interested in catching a late dinner or show at one of the area's restaurants, bars and theaters. Burying her chin in the folds of her scarf, she hurried along the sidewalk.

Passing a group of carolers left her humming a favorite carol. A horse-drawn carriage, its passengers bundled up beneath layers of blankets and snapping pictures of the mosaics, frescoes and bronze statues decorating the Mediterranean architecture, made her smile. The oohs and applause from a group of shoppers gathered in front of an animated store window convinced Beth to stop and watch the show for herself.

Elf-size robots with rosy cheeks and pointed hats came to life beneath a tree decorated with white lights and crystal ornaments. The first one set a shiny package beneath the tree and opened the lid. Beth joined the gasps of delight as a stuffed pony waddled out, followed by a colorful train engine. As they took their place beneath the tree, the second elf opened his gift.

A young couple moved through the crowd, jostling against Beth's back. She felt a tug at her purse strap and instinctively hugged her bag to her chest. "Hey!"

"Sorry." Pickpockets enjoyed the influx of shoppers as much as the area's business owners did. But the woman smiled and the man apologized before plunging farther into the storefront audience.

A quick check showed her purse was still latched. But Beth didn't relax her posture. After the couple's disruption, the twenty or so people standing around her seemed to be jockeying for position, bumping her again. A small boy, sitting on his father's shoulders, moved in front of her, blocking her view of the window. A touch, as light as the breeze and just as chilling, brushed across her back. Another round of applause drowned out her protest.

That was it. She was done. The holiday magic had ended for her. She was going home.

When Beth turned, she caught a glimpse of a big man standing at the fringe of the crowd near the street. For one telling moment, her lips creased with a smile. Kevin. He'd come, anyway.

But just as quickly, her smile vanished. The man was already walking away from her, pulling a cap over hair that was brown, not the color of golden wheat. Definitely not Kevin.

Muttering a curse at the foolish paranoia that had consumed her from the moment she'd hit her head, Beth hustled her boots on down the sidewalk toward the 47th Street parking garage. Six steps, seven. Her subconscious mind screamed at her to stop.

Black wool coat. Black stocking cap.

She spun around, looked back at the crowd. But the man was gone.

No, no, no, no, no. He couldn't just disappear like that. Beth stretched up on her toes and scanned the pedestrians in front of the store. But there was too much movement, too many people, to see beyond the first few standing between her and the man. She hurried to the edge of the sidewalk to peer between cars parked at the curb. Her gaze darted up and down the street. He could have gone into a store, climbed inside a vehicle.

But she knew he was hiding, watching her right now.

Why? What had she done? What did he want with her?

"Ma'am?" Beth jerked her attention to the woman's voice at her side. "Did you lose someone?"

Then again, maybe she was the only one paying too much attention to the other people around her.

"No." Beth dredged up a smile. Holding a little girl in her arms, the woman probably thought Beth had lost a child. "I'm fine. I just couldn't remember where I parked." She came up with the quickest lie she could think of. "I thought it might have been towed, but I remember now. Thanks."

"Merry Christmas."

"Merry…Christmas." It was a lousy delivery to a kind soul who'd only been trying to help. She waved to the little girl as they walked away.

Before she dropped her hand, Beth touched her gloved fingers to the edge of the bandage in her hair and massaged around the spot, easing the phantom pain that suddenly throbbed there.

She was crazy. That was it. She was crazy from lack of sleep and stress at work. "Just go home," Beth advised herself. "Just go home."

Bracing her resolve against the cold and her irrational fears, Beth quickened her pace. The crowd thinned as she left the shops and night spots behind and crossed over to the block housing the parking garage. Soon she was no longer weaving between strolling couples and nighttime revelers. And by the time she passed around the garage's automated entry gate, the trio of shoppers she'd been trailing had opened the trunk of their car to load their packages inside. With a polite nod, they climbed into the car and Beth was left to walk the rest of the way to her Jeep alone.

Or not.

A flurry of movement from the corner of her eye drew her attention. Beth turned, looked. Breathed again. Just the wind catching a drift of snow and blowing it through the sidewalk railing into the garage.

Yet Beth's imagination wouldn't let it go. She had that feeling again. Interested eyes boring holes into her back. Unblinking. Watching.

"Stop it." No one had followed her into the bookstore. No one was following her now.

But the quick thump of her heart couldn't drown out the scrape of footsteps on the concrete a few yards behind her.

Beth picked up her pace, pulling her keys from her pocket and locking them between her fingers. A quick three-sixty revealed nothing but cars and concrete and the street beyond. *Keep walking.*

Thankfully, she'd found a spot on the ground level, but it was on the third row in, farther from the sidewalk and the crowds. The footsteps kept pace with her stride, but there was no one behind her. She reached the striped crosswalk leading to the back rows and crossed to the next driving lane between parking spaces.

Another whisper of movement, darker than snow, stopped her in her tracks.

Black coat. Black stocking cap. Dark eyes. A faceless figure walking straight down the middle of the driving lane. Toward her.

Her Jeep was right there, four cars away.

But the dark figure kept coming. She could get inside, lock her doors.

No. Not enough time. Beth quickly reversed course.

The footsteps followed.

"Help!" Fear poured into her veins. She broke into a jog, shouted through the echoing steel and concrete. "Help me!"

Ignoring crosswalks and warning signs, she zigzagged through the cars and ran straight for the railing at the edge of the garage.

The footsteps grew louder, moved faster.

Beth hoisted herself up onto the railing, swung her legs over. The shadow rushed up behind her as she dropped down onto the other side. The frozen sidewalk jolted through her shins and knees, throwing her off balance. But the pain was irrelevant. She forgot her bag, ignored her purse, pushed to her feet.

Head for the lights. Find people. Run.

"Beth?"

Oof! She smacked right into a wall of tan wool and tweed.

She shoved herself back, opened her mouth to scream. But a wonderful smell—of musk and man—and the familiar contour of a once-broken nose stole the sound from her throat.

"Kev?" She mouthed the word, her relief so intense she felt lightheaded.

"You want to tell me what those phone calls…?"

Beth never heard the rest of the question. She thrust her hands inside his coat and wrapped her arms around Kevin's waist, pulling herself closer and closer, until she could bury her nose in the nubby weave of his jacket and feel the heat of his body.

She couldn't hear the footsteps behind her anymore— only her own frantic breathing and the steady beat of Kevin's heart beneath her ear.

"So that rule about not grabbing only goes one way…. Well, hell, lady." She felt the stiffness leave his body more than she heard his surrendering sigh. He folded his arms around her and lowered his chin to the crown of her hair, sealing her in a cocoon of strength and warmth. "It's nothing, my ass."

KEVIN WONDERED IF HE WAS ever going to lose the imprint of Beth Rogers's body clinging to his. She'd been a perfect fit with her arms wound around him, her head tucked beneath his chin.

She'd trembled against him, smelling of cold and garage fumes and fear. She'd held on to him as if her life depended on it, clutching fistfuls of his jacket and shirt at the middle of his back. And when he'd cupped his hand behind her head and tried to ease some space between them, she'd burrowed against his heart and held on even more tightly.

Even through the bulk of her coat and clothes, he'd felt breasts and hips and needy fingers. Her breathing evened out and she whispered his name. Once. Twice. When she did finally pull away, she looked straight up into his eyes and said, "I'm so happy to see you."

Then, when they went to pick up the items she'd dropped and find out what had spooked her, she took one of his hands and held on with both of hers. Every step of the way.

Heady stuff for a man whose last physical encounters with women had involved fainting and a slap in the face.

"You've ruined me, Grove," Sheila had accused outside the private hearing room. *"I*

could lose my license to practice law because of what you said in that hearing."

"You ruined us," Kevin had stated matter-of-factly, refusing to waste one more emotion. "You damn well ruined me."

Sheila Mercer was still practicing law. Kevin Grove no longer had faith in women or relationships. Not anymore.

But looking across the table at Café Geno's into the animated features and wholesome beauty of Beth Rogers, he wished he could trust what he was feeling right now.

There was certainly a logical explanation for clutching and snuggling and *"Hold me, please."* Even though he'd seen no one in the deserted garage after she finally explained what she'd been running from, Beth's fear had been real enough. He wore a badge. He was solid. And he was there. Reasons enough for a pretty woman to want to cling to him.

He just had to remember that it was a matter of luck that had made her turn to him twice in two days. She'd needed a cop, needed an ally—and he just happened to be the guy who'd shown up at the right place at the right time. And she seemed to be a genuinely nice person—polite enough to offer to buy him a cup of coffee as a way of saying thanks tonight. She'd invited him to Café Geno's, probably as much to give herself a chance to warm up and get her rattled nerves back under control, as to repay him for showing up when she had no one else in the city to turn to.

No matter how his senses sharpened into focus around Beth Rogers, no matter how his body perked up the way any other healthy man's would when she threw all those curves against him—no matter how something territorial and protective thrummed through his veins at the notion of another man harming or terrorizing her—he'd be a fool if he thought the soft smiles and hot coffee meant anything more than neighborly friendship or gratitude. And Kevin Grove was no fool.

When the waitress came to their booth and dropped off their ticket, Kevin automatically reached for it. Keeping the whole "friendship only" caveat in mind, he intended to go dutch treat.

Beth reached across the table and lightly smacked the back of his knuckles, pulling the ticket from his fingers. "I said I was paying."

"You invited me for coffee. Not the slice of pumpkin pie I demolished along with it."

"Are you kidding me?" She pulled her purse onto her lap and dug through the deep, accordion-fold pockets. "You think I can't afford coffee *and* pie?"

"I didn't want to overstep my limits or make you think this was some kind of—" *date.*

"Oh, Lordy." She paused the search and frowned at him. "I'm sorry. I should have offered you dinner, not a snack. A big man like you? You were working, weren't you. You probably haven't eaten since lunch."

"Try breakfast." Her eyes rounded, but he put up his hands and silenced her before she could get out another apology. "I'm not complaining. Trust me, between moving and work, I haven't been eating dinner until late at night anyway." He pushed aside his empty plate. "This pie *was* my lunch."

"Great. Now I feel really guilty." She dived back into her purse to retrieve her wallet and straighten the items left behind. "I suppose I'll have to cook you a meal."

"I wasn't hinting—"

"I don't do gourmet or anything, but my brothers think I'm pretty good."

"You don't have to—"

"Do you like cookies? That's usually how I repay Hank when he rakes leaves or clears my sidewalk and driveway. That old man has such a…sweet tooth." Her hands and mouth suddenly stilled. Twin lines of confusion appeared between her brows.

Answering a concern he didn't want to feel, Kevin braced his elbows on the edge of the table and leaned in. "Beth?"

Holding it by the key ring attached to it, she pulled a small, black plastic computer memory stick from inside her purse and held it up for him to see. "I think someone's trying to gaslight me."

Gaslight as in make her think she was crazy? "Why do you say that?"

She dropped the flash drive onto the table as if the key ring had given her a tiny shock. "That wasn't in my bag an hour ago—not when I checked out of the bookstore." She shoved it farther away and withdrew to hug her arms around her purse. "When I stopped to watch the window display at Harzfeld's, I got bumped in the crowd and thought someone was trying to rob me. I checked to see that my wallet was still there and then I left. Instead of taking something, whoever it was must have slipped this into the outside pocket."

"That's not yours?"

"No."

Kevin used his napkin to pick it up by the key ring and dangled it beneath the light over their table. Beyond the manufacturer's logo, there were no markings. He couldn't even tell if it held music, data or anything at all. "Did you see anyone suspicious?"

"I don't know. There was a younger couple. The man with the black coat and hat."

"Who followed you into the garage?"

"Who must be a figment of my imagination because nobody else saw him." With a disgusted huff, she sank back in her seat. "Not even you."

Ignoring the subtle gibe at his earlier skepticism, Kevin inspected the tiny device from every angle. If there were prints to be had, he couldn't see them. "Do you think this came from the same man who attacked you?"

"I don't know. There were so many people in the crowd. I suppose anyone could have put it there."

"And you don't recognize it?"

"No, I…" Energized by a sudden thought, she sat forward and snatched the case from his hand. "My boss said he'd misplaced a flash drive at work. This is the same brand we use—but the one he wanted would have been labeled. Besides, I turned my office inside out looking for it after lunch…" Her energy dissipated along with the sparkle in her eyes.

"What?"

She slid the memory stick back into the outside pocket of her purse and, for a moment, Kevin thought she wasn't going to give him the explanation he'd demanded. "I almost called you this afternoon. I think someone searched through my office some time last night or this morning."

"Why didn't you tell me?"

"I knew you were at work, that I was a pest and that you didn't get much sleep last night." She shrugged and reached for her mug of coffee with cream. "Anyway, I finally decided my boss must have gone through my desk and files looking for the electronic copy of the research he misplaced." Cradling the mug between her hands, Beth took a sip. "He's been acting kind of weird lately."

"Weird, how?"

"Absent-minded. Troubled." Her peach-colored lips parted to tell him more. But then she smiled away the barrage of questions he'd been asking. "You work major cases, remember? You don't have to solve anything for the crazy lady next door who imagines things. After last night, apparently anything and everything frightens me."

"Listen, lady." When Kevin lowered his voice and leaned in, her eyes dilated. With anticipation? Attraction? Fear? But to her credit, the woman didn't back away. "I worked two homicides today. Two old men with their guts cut out of them. You've got no idea what crazy is. Now talk to me."

Her soft gasp was the only warning he had before she reached out and covered his hand where it rested on the table. "Kev, that's awful. I'm so sorry. Are you all right? If people are dead, you shouldn't be worrying about me."

Was *he* all right? Hell, he'd just been doing his job. Still, the chatter of the other customers, the bustle of waitresses hurrying past, faded to a pair of compassionate gray-blue eyes and a strong, warm hand covering his own meaty paw.

"Can't help worrying." He'd already revealed more than he should. What harm could there be in twisting his fingers to squeeze her hand before pulling away? "So quit wasting my time and talk."

She answered his intimate touch with a sweet smile and the hard places around his heart began to turn to mush. *Tough guy. Ha.* His conscience mocked him, but he ignored the internal taunt and steeled his gaze, suspecting the hardening of his expression wasn't putting her off the way he intended. Certainly, nothing was stopping her mouth or the nimble way she steepled and laced and busied her hands while she talked. He wondered if it was nerves or excess energy that made those hands so eager to move and touch.

He wondered what it would feel like to have those supple fingers dancing across more than the tough skin of his hand.

Well, hell. Kevin shifted in his seat, putting the kibosh on the interest stirring south of his belt buckle.

Once he'd settled again, he listened silently as Beth recounted her boss's freak-out over the missing drug research data, and the odd sense that she was being targeted somehow—though for what reason, she couldn't say. "I wonder, if someone thought *I* had taken that research out of the office, then that could explain going through my clothes and purse when I was unconscious. My attacker was trying to retrieve it."

"What's wrong with the research?"

"What's wrong?" She bristled up, curling her fingers into fists. "Nothing's wrong. Dr. Landon needs the data for our semi-annual board meeting. GlennCo is a successful, reputable company. We do thorough clinical trials on every drug before we put it on the market."

"That's the company line. Is your Dr. Landon in the habit of accusing you of theft when he can't find things?"

"No."

He could see that loyalty to GlennCo, or at least to her boss, ran pretty deep. "If there's no problem, then there's no need to nearly kill you to get that information back."

"He didn't try to kill—"

"Somebody did. You passed out in my arms, lady. You could have bled out or suffered a brain hemorrhage if you hadn't had the gumption to drag yourself through the snow to my front porch." Kevin drank the last of his coffee and set the mug on the table, still holding it as he made his point. "I told you I don't mince words."

"I can appreciate honesty, but you know, sometimes you scare me."

"I scare a lot of people."

Her exasperated sigh whispered clear across the table. "I think you do it on purpose. So people don't see there might be a nice guy lurking beneath the surface. Didn't anyone ever teach you subtlety? Or manners?"

Kevin released the mug and leaned back against the bench seat. "My grandma taught me how to get along with people just fine."

Her eyebrows arched with surprise. "You have a grandmother?"

"No, I was spawned from a puddle of goo." Beth laughed. Not his intention, but for a moment, Kevin figured he must be a pretty good guy to make her do so. This was dangerous ground he was walking on with her. Despite the traitorous clench of muscles on either side of his mouth, he should not, could not, share in her laughter. "Yes, I have a grandmother. She's in a nursing home. She took care of me when my mother left. Now I take care of her."

"See? You're not so tough, Kevin Grove. You have a sense of humor." She opened her wallet and set her money with the ticket at the edge of the table, continuing the conversation as if they had a reason to get better acquainted that went beyond late-night attacks and missing flash drives and his own growing certainty that nothing Beth had shared had been a figment of a skittish imagination. "This grandmother raised you?"

"Taught me to be honest, straightforward—be a man."

"She succeeded. Maybe you could use a little refinement around the edges, but she sounds remarkable."

"Miriam is." Few people in the world would believe how 98 pounds of sass and love and a strict set of rules could turn an unwanted boy into a 250 pound man who put away bad guys for a living. "I've also learned the hard way that, um…" Well, hell. Why was he telling her this? But the words came out, unfiltered, anyway. "I'm pretty blunt because I don't want anything I say or do to ever be misconstrued again."

"What does that mean?"

"Earlier this year, I was brought up on suspicion of sexual harassment at work."

"You?"

A charmer like him, huh? Go figure. "A woman I used to date, an attorney—she reported me to Internal Affairs—said I'd forced her into a relationship in order to exchange information about a perp she was defending."

"Did you? Force her, I mean?"

He looked Beth dead in the eye, any impulse to laugh wisely eradicated. "Sheila was the one using me. Figured I was an easy way into the department because I don't…"

"Date a lot?"

Yeah. He should have been a smarter detective when Sheila Mercer had first come on to him during the Pekoe investigation. "When I found out she was using pillow talk to promote her case and get her client off, I called her on it."

"And she retaliated by accusing you of harassment."

"It put a mark on my record. Cost me the

trust and respect of some of the men and women I serve with."

It looked like he'd successfully wiped away any lingering urge for Beth to keep smiling at him. "Your job is important to you, isn't it?"

"It's everything." It was the one place where looks and charm—or lack thereof—didn't get in the way of succeeding. "So when I tell you I want to know the facts, I'm not making polite conversation."

"And when you come to my rescue time and again? Is that just part of your job, too?"

Sliding to the edge of the seat, Kevin stood up and grabbed his coat. Touchy-feely time was over. He'd better go back to thinking like a cop around Beth Rogers before things became any more personal and he got himself well and truly screwed again. "Pay the bill. I'll walk you to your car and follow you home."

An hour later, Kevin had completed his walk-through of Beth's house. There were touches of color and personalization here and there as she gradually transformed a beige and blah house into a home of her own. But despite the cleanliness, modern conveniences and homey touches, there was still something about the place that didn't seem quite right.

Beth must have picked up on his suspicions as soon as he joined her in the living room. She hugged her arms around her waist and tilted her chin. "You're brooding again. Is something wrong?"

He wouldn't speculate when he couldn't say exactly what it was about the house that didn't fit. "I see you put your computer back together in your office."

"I haven't had time to clean up everything in there. But I needed to send an e-mail."

He nodded his head toward the dining area and the boarded-up French doors there. "Can't say I'm thrilled that you haven't gotten those replaced yet."

"I really can't do anything until the weekend," she explained. "Unless I hire someone to do it while I'm at work. And I'm not really keen on having another stranger in my house."

"I don't blame you." Kevin nodded and crossed through the dining room to check the security of the two-by-fours and plastic tarp again. "Maybe I can get over here tomorrow after work." He inspected what was left of the hinges beneath the tarp. "I've got some lumber in my garage left over from redoing the upstairs bath. I could—"

"No." He jumped at the touch of her hand on his arm, then covered the startle by immediately circling around the oak table and heading for the front door. "You've done enough already. I won't ask you to play carpenter for me, too."

"You didn't ask. I volunteered." He unlocked the dead bolt and paused with his hand on the door knob. "Get that door fixed tomorrow night or I'll be over here to do it for you."

"You're being bossy again."

"You're being stubborn." He normally wasn't the type to lose two nights of sleep in a row over any woman. But he suspected he'd be up at his window, watching over her as long as he thought there was any chance someone could get to her and harm her again. "If you want, I can leave Daisy out in her dog house tonight. She'll raise a ruckus if anyone's prowling around the back of your house."

"Are you kidding? Keep her inside where

it's warm." He felt her fingers at the back of his collar, turning it up before he went out into the night. "I'll be safe. I've got a cop next door, right?"

Kevin opened the door to a blast of cold air and stepped down onto the first brick step of her porch before he turned, blocking the storm door open with his shoulder and bracing a hand against the jamb. "Lock that behind me. Don't open it for anybody you don't know. Call me if anything—"

"—bothers me. I know."

He couldn't take his eyes off that soft, peachy smile. "Bossy enough for you?"

"I'm beginning to think that *bossy* means you care." The wind had already pinked her undamaged cheek when she unwound her arms and braced a hand against his chest. "Thanks, Kev." And then she was stretching onto her toes, moving closer—pressing the gentlest of kisses to the grizzled angle of his jaw. "For everything."

She sank back onto her heels, but the hand stayed. His blood pumped faster, rushing to warm the spot where she touched him. Their eyes locked. Breaths mingled. Kevin breathed in vanilla and spice and pure temptation, and couldn't find the strength to retreat one inch as she leaned in a second time and brushed her lips across his.

Don't do this. A voice inside his head tried to argue with his feverish pulse. *Move.*

But he couldn't hear the voice over the pent-up desire whooshing inside his ears. Her other hand found its way beneath the collar of his coat. Beth was holding on to him, tugging at him. He took her weight as she pulled herself up and kissed him again. More firmly this time, pulling his bottom lip between hers, stroking it with the tip of her tongue.

Kevin watched her long sable lashes drift against her cheeks as Beth closed her eyes and stretched up another half inch to firmly suckle that bottom lip. The shyly decadent movement shot a bullet of want straight down to his groin. Well, hell. The need, the want, the loneliness too long denied shuddered through him and Kevin could no longer walk away nor resist. With his hands gripping the doorframe on either side of her, he parted his lips, quickly changing her tentative exploration into his own bold claim.

Beth had to curl her fingers into his lapels

and hold on as he drove his lips against hers and thrust his tongue inside her mouth. Kevin pushed her back half a step with the force of his kiss, feeling a little off balance himself when he heard the moan in her throat and felt her tongue slide against his. The wind chill outside had plummeted into negative degrees, but Kevin was feeling nothing but heat. He tasted the coffee on her tongue, the scorching sweetness of her lips, the generosity of her response. And he wanted more.

There was nothing suave about his kiss. Nothing patient or tender or any other damn dumb thing but fire and passion and feeling like a man again. And hang it all, but freckle-faced Beth Rogers was winding her hands up behind his neck and holding on to join him in the conflagration.

Stop. The voice in his head tried to warn him away even as he shucked a glove and threaded his fingers into the velvety soft hair at her nape. He wanted to pull her against his body, feel her curves melting into all the hard places that craved an honest, passionate touch. *You're taking advantage of her. The woman's just too nice to tell you to take a hike.*

That cruel self-doubt, ingrained long before Sheila Mercer and a harassment suit made him wonder if there'd ever be a woman in his life beyond friends and one-night stands and an eighty-two-year-old grandmother who loved him unconditionally, finally got him to wake up and wise up and stop acting with his zipper instead of his brain. Beth Rogers needed something from him, but it wasn't this.

Reaching up, Kevin grasped Beth's wrists and pulled them from his neck. With a mighty burst of self-preserving control, he tore his mouth from hers and set her firmly away from him.

A blessed rush of freezing air whipped around him, cooling the fire in his blood and frosting each heated breath that filled the space between them. With the dim light from the porch lamp to illuminate her pale face, her eyes narrowed, questioned him. Her lips were swollen and sexy and pursed to do verbal battle with him again. But there was no way he was arguing this time. He scooped up his glove from the snow-dusted bricks and yanked it on. "You already said thank you. I'm not asking you to do anything more."

"You think that was…?" She huffed in disgust and grabbed his coat, stopping him from turning away. "What if I wanted to kiss you?"

He had to blame that raspy catch in her voice on the cold. "You expect me to believe that you're turned on by me?"

"There's more to admire about a man than his face."

He disengaged her hands a second time. "So you admit I'm an ugly SOB."

"I didn't say—"

"I'm built like a freight train and I carry a gun. That's got to make you feel safer than you did before you met me. I get that."

"I'm attracted to you, Kevin. Maybe you're not like any man I've dated before, but I'm not trying to buy your protection with a kiss." She gave him a little shake before pulling away and hugging her arms around her waist again. "I wouldn't complain if you decided you were attracted to me, too, and wanted to do something about it."

"Funny." He stepped off the porch, not feeling one whit like laughing. "That's what Sheila said to me. Lock the damn door. Good night."

Chapter Six

"I thought you said you'd handled it!" He stormed into the meeting room, tossing his coat and gloves on the back of a chair and heading straight for the liquor cabinet.

The big man rose from his chair, looking uncharacteristically startled by the accusation. "I did. I got the disk back from that woman. And I shredded the document, just like you ordered."

He poured himself two fingers of bourbon, swallowed it down and poured himself another before he turned to glare at the old man sitting at the opposite end of the table. "Apparently, another copy of your *conscience* is still out there somewhere. Did anyone else get a special delivery this evening?"

"Yes." The big man pulled a matching envelope from his pocket.

The woman tossed hers onto the table. "No handwriting, no return address, no idea who's behind this."

Surprisingly enough, the old man pulled out a letter, as well. "We all got them. I don't understand. It isn't supposed to happen this way."

The woman's sarcasm was cutting. "Did you have some other plan in mind for bilking us out of millions of dollars?"

"I'm telling you, I didn't send these. Profiting from our mistakes was never part of my plan."

"Yet someone *is* profiting from our work." The man in charge polished off his second glass before facing the group again. The fire in his belly matched the sense of betrayal that burned through him. He unbuttoned his collar and loosened his tie before taking his place at the head of the table.

He waited for the others to sit, eyeing each of them around the table, trying to assess which one of them was lying to him. The old man was the obvious choice, but he looked drawn and devastated and frankly incapable of playing such a tough game. The big man? He'd have the guts to do it, but even if his allegiance had shifted, he'd be surprised if his enforcer had the forethought to pull it off. The woman? Now she'd have the brains to conceive of such a plan—turning an information leak that could ruin them all into an opportunity to make herself a tidy fortune. Although he'd been certain he'd bought her loyalty in the bedroom. Besides, she had plenty of other weapons in her arsenal to get what she wanted which were more effective and less crass than a blackmail letter.

Time to get the facts and put a stop to all this posturing nonsense. "Is there anyone outside this room who knows about the clinical trial results and the cover-up solution I authorized?"

The old man nodded. "Dr. Allen in the lab suspects something. Although when I met with him, he didn't show me any proof—he merely raised concerns about moving Gehirn 330 into production so quickly." He paused until he had everyone's attention. "I have a solution. If we go public with this—"

"Absolutely not!" the woman snapped.

"If we go public," he repeated more slowly, "then that takes the leverage away from our blackmailer. Yes, there'd be legal consequences for us to face, fines to pay—"

The big man shot to his feet. "Some of us would have to face a lot more than a fine. If it comes down to it, I won't be the only one going to prison, I promise you."

The man at the head of the table pounded his glass like a gavel. He didn't appreciate being included in his hireling's threat. "No one's going to jail. No one's paying a fine—or blackmail. And no one's taking my business from me."

"*Our* business, don't you mean?" The old man had the guts to challenge him after all. "I think we can confess our sins and still salvage the company. The work we've done over the years far outweighs this mistake."

He shook his head. "Running a 'salvaged' company isn't exactly how I planned to go into retirement." He opened the drawer to the liquor cabinet and retrieved a set of keys to unlock the doors below. He pulled out a manila envelope and handed it to the big man to open and examine the photographs and transcriptions inside. "Pass them around. I think you'll all find them very interesting."

Impatient to see the information, the woman stood and reached across the table to snatch one of the printouts. She frowned.

"This shows repeated attempts to access our company server and hack into encrypted files." She handed the information to the old man. "Is there any way to know if the user was successful?"

"You got a blackmail letter, didn't you?" the big man scoffed. "That could be our info link."

"No." The old man stood at the far end of the table, holding a printout and a photograph.

"I picked that up off surveillance last night."

"How did you get these pictures? You can't have had a warrant to authorize spying like this."

When it came to protecting what was his, legalities didn't matter. "I just followed the trail you laid out for us."

The old man shook his head, refusing to believe what was right in front of his eyes. "She knows nothing about this. If she did, she wouldn't be blackmailing *me*."

The evidence wasn't conclusive, but the story it told made a hell of a lot of sense. "Are you sure any woman can be that loyal to you?"

The old man's eyes met the woman's gaze. Now there was an example of loyalty gone sideways. If he'd been in a better mood, he'd have laughed to see how the old man wilted back into his chair.

The old man shook his head. "I can't do this anymore. I'm turning in my resignation at the board meeting tomorrow. I can't afford the money. My heart can't afford the stress. If it would ease everyone's concerns, I'm happy to retire to a country that doesn't have extradition to the U.S. And I'm happy to keep my mouth shut."

"You expect us to take your word for that?" The big man paced in front of the windows.

The old man turned to the head of the table. "Once upon a time, my word was good enough for you."

For a moment, the man in charge was taken back in time, to when they were both young entrepreneurs carving out a rather large niche for themselves in the world. "Once upon a time you wouldn't have betrayed me, either."

"You're the one who's betrayed us all."

The old man had had the vision—and the brains to develop many of the patents that made them a success. But *he* knew how to run a business and how to make money—a lot of money. The old man would still be slaving away in a lab, earning respectable wages. But because *he* was a good boss, he'd made them both rich.

And a good boss—as he'd learned long ago—knew how to delegate. He looked to each person in the room. "Someone needs to make this problem go away. Find the black-mailer. Retrieve the information. Make it stop." He needed another drink. "And I don't care how you do it."

"KEVIN ELIJAH GROVE, what are you doing here?"

Getting firmly grounded back in the reality of my life. "I came to have breakfast with my best girl."

Kevin quickly covered the distance of the Oak Park Retirement Care Center's sun porch and leaned down to kiss his grand-mother's papery-thin cheek. Miriam Grove released her walker and hugged a frail arm around her grandson's neck. Kevin lightly touched his palms to her back. As much as he loved this woman, he couldn't give her a real hug anymore, fearing that the combination of his strength and her osteoporosis would result in a broken bone if he wasn't careful.

She, however, had no qualms about sharing the love. Pulling back, she cupped his jaw, clucking her tongue behind her teeth as she inspected his face. "You haven't been getting enough sleep."

He covered her hand with his and smiled. "You know there are days when I have to work long hours."

"Uh-huh," she agreed in a dubious tone. "Come, sit with me." She turned with her walker and slowly made her way to one of the flowered love seats facing each other in the window-lined solarium. "The nurse wanted to bring me a tray in my room. Can you believe it? What's the point of getting up in the morning if you don't actually 'get up' out of bed?"

"Now, now, Miriam, I thought I was being nice." A middle-aged African-American woman in a light blue staff uniform entered the room, carrying a tray of scrambled eggs, toast and a can of nutrient supplement. "I only asked because so many of our residents prefer to stay in their warm beds when it's this cold outside." She shivered as the windows rattled. "I feel that wind go right through me, even if you don't. Good morning, Detective Grove."

"Good morning, Yolanda." Kevin braced his arm for his grandmother to hold on to while she lowered herself down into the sofa cushions. "Is Miriam being a handful today?"

Yolanda winked as she moved the walker and set up a folding TV tray in its place. "Miriam is a handful every day. She keeps me on my toes."

Kevin could imagine. Miriam's strong will had gotten the best of him for thirty-seven years now. He chuckled as he moved aside for the nurse's aide to get his grandmother situated.

"That's why I like her. The days I work with your grandmother are never boring. There." Yolanda finished opening the nutrient supplement and tucking a napkin into the neckline of Miriam's robe. "Could I get you a cup of coffee, detective?"

"I'm good."

Yolanda pointed to the coffee pot and paper cups on the table between a decorated Christmas tree and the sunporch's arched entryway. "If you change your mind, it's right there. There's sugar, cream, whatever you need."

"Thanks."

Yolanda slid her hands into the pockets of her jacket and excused herself. "I'd better finish my rounds. Mr. Del Ray gets extra cranky if his meals are late." She pointed to Miriam's plate before heading through the archway. "Now clean your plate. At the very least, drink the supplement. You need your calcium."

"Bossy boots," Miriam muttered.

"Sunshine," Yolanda shot back as she left.

Both women were smiling.

"I'm beginning to think that bossy means you care."

Beth Rogers's teasing voice interrupted Kevin's thoughts the same way their kiss had haunted his dreams last night. The hell of it was that he *was* beginning to care about the freckle-faced brunette. No wonder he was getting circles under his eyes. Between worrying over her safety, unraveling the mystery of the odd events surrounding her these past two nights—and lusting after her even though common sense told him that her willingness to kiss and cling never would have happened if she hadn't been in danger—he was guaranteed plenty of sleepless nights.

There was no way to break the curse of his size and face, or dissolve the distrust that encased his heart. And there was no way to have a real relationship with a woman unless he could.

"Sit down, son." A tug on his coat sleeve brought Kevin back to the Oak Park solarium and the chiding voice of his grandmother. "When you tower over me like that, it makes me feel short."

"You *are* short."

She pointed a knobby finger at him. "I hope you don't talk to all the girls in your life with that smart mouth."

Kevin snorted. *All* the girls? "I'm supposed to lie to them?"

"No, but when you love someone, you see them differently than the rest of the world does."

He pulled off his coat and draped it over the back of the love seat. "Is that why I think you're such a beauty?"

Sharp as a tack, she didn't miss the perfect setup line. "I *am* a beauty." When Kevin laughed, she tried to take advantage of his good humor. "Before you sit down, go get me a cup of coffee. Yolanda forgot to bring me one."

Kevin sat anyway. "She didn't forget. You know caffeine isn't in your diet. The doctor says it keeps your bones from absorbing the calcium they need."

"Oh, but it smells so good." With a resigned shrug of her thin shoulders, she stabbed a forkful of eggs and ate a bite. "Mr. Harrison would get his morning coffee, take his pills and come sit with me out here every morning while I ate. I enjoyed the smell of his coffee as much as I enjoyed the conversation."

"Who's Mr. Harrison?" Kevin asked.

"*Was,*" she amended sadly. After swallowing another bite, she set down her fork and gazed out the floor-to-ceiling windows. With the winter storm having moved on, the sky was clear. Although it did little to warm the temperature outside, the sun shone brightly, illuminating crystals of light over the carpet of new-fallen snow. "He was quite the gardener. Don't know if that's what he did before retirement, but he always sounded so knowledgeable. He was suffering from the onset of senility. His son or daughter would visit from time to time, and though he couldn't seem to remember their names or faces, he could identify every plant in the garden. He was a talented artist, too. He'd draw sketches of how he thought the court-yard and garden would look when the flowers were all in bloom."

Kevin reached over to pat Miriam's hand. "When did he pass?"

Growing a little agitated, she picked up her fork and poked her eggs around her plate. "I'm not sure. Last week sometime? When you get to be my age, you aren't surprised when you lose a friend. I'd like to send a card to his children or buy some flowers for his grave, but the staff here won't tell me anything."

"They're protecting your feelings," Kevin suggested.

"I don't want protection, I want to honor a man who became my friend this past year."

"I'll ask Yolanda if she knows anything before I leave."

Although a little on the wistful side, Miriam's smile returned. "Thank you, dear. The last morning I saw Mr. Harrison, he talked about how the groundskeeper should already be preparing the dirt for planting in the spring—to take advantage of the moisture all this snow provides. Through his eyes I could picture the roses and irises blooming already."

Knowing how his grandmother had loved the flowers in her own garden, Kevin could well imagine how she'd enjoyed Mr. Harrison's company. "I'm sure he looked forward to your mornings together, too."

"He complained of stomach gripes that last morning." Miriam shook her head. "It's like he just disappeared. I went down to his room, but everything that was his had already been packed up. Sent to his children, I suppose. But I wouldn't have minded keeping one of those sketches."

He'd be sure to ask about that, too.

"Enough about me." She patted Kevin's knee on the seat beside her. "You didn't come to hear me go on. Tell me what's troubling you, dear."

"Nothing's troubling me."

"Something's up." She squeezed his knee. "Where do you think you learned your deductive reasoning skills?"

"The police academy?"

But he wasn't joking his way out of this one. "Is it a case?"

"I'm working a couple of tough ones right now," he admitted. "But I'm handling them."

"Then what's causing those shadows under your eyes? Are you ill? Is it a woman?"

"No and no."

Kevin didn't think he'd even blinked. But Miriam's expression lit up with a smile. "It *is* a woman. What's her name? Is she nice? She treats you better than that last witch did, doesn't she?"

"How do you…?" He shook his head, realizing he'd just been outted by the master. "Beth's no witch."

"Beth, is it?"

"I'm not telling you anything because there's nothing to tell."

"Have you kissed her yet?"

"Grandma!"

"You have." She clapped her hands together.

"I'm not discussing this with you."

If her age would let her, Miriam would be sliding across the love seat and shaking the answers out of him. "I can't be your best girl, forever, Kevin. I want you to find someone."

"You're not planning on going anywhere anytime soon, are you?"

With a frustrated sigh, Miriam's excitement dissipated. "That dog you rescued won't be company enough for you when I'm gone. You need a woman. You need babies."

"Grandma—"

"Just remember that you are the finest man I know. If she can't see that…"

Then Beth would be no different than the other women he'd been attracted to in his life. "She's in a little trouble. I'm trying to help."

"Well, that's something, anyway. I always expect you to do the right thing. Even if it's hard."

Being a good neighbor was turning out to be harder than he'd ever imagined. "Even if it means walking away from a relationship that shouldn't happen and can't last?"

Miriam frowned. "That's that witch talking. She was blind not to see the prince inside you. Don't let what she did to you spoil your ability to fall in love again. Is Beth important to you, Kevin?"

"I've known her for only two days."

"I knew you were important the moment

your mother left you on my kitchen table. I
didn't need two days to fall in love with you."
Miriam articulated the words as if he hadn't
understood them. "Is Beth important?"

Apparently, the answer he wasn't sure of
was written plainly on his face. With a
soothing maternal smile, Miriam reached up
and cupped his cheek. "I know you have a
good heart, son. The right woman will accept
you as you are and love you just as much as
I do. But you have to be brave enough to
give her a chance."

He covered her precious hand with his
own. "Man up and risk putting it all out
there, hmm?"

"If that means what I think it does, then
yes." She pulled away and went back to
picking at her breakfast. "Bring her by to
meet me sometime. I'll check her out and tell
you if she's good enough for you. Now
couldn't I have just a teensy-bitty sip of
coffee?"

Miriam's advice about pursuing a relationship with Beth wasn't the only disturbing information Kevin got at the Oak Park Center
that morning. He stopped at the front desk on
his way out to ask Yolanda about contacting

Mr. Harrison's children to try to track down a memento for his grandmother.

Yolanda frowned at the request. "Mr. Harrison didn't have any children. He was never even married that I know of."

"But my grandmother said a son and daughter came to visit him."

"The only visitors Mr. Harrison ever had were his doctors. That was because he was part of a clinical drug trial to slow down and reverse his Alzheimer's. From what I could tell from the year he was here was that the drug was succeeding. He had more good days than bad toward the end."

"What did Mr. Harrison die of?"

"Old age, I suppose. He died in his sleep. His doctors claimed the body for a medical autopsy to complete their research—it was all set up in Mr. Harrison's will. I haven't heard any results."

"Do you know who was conducting the research?"

"GlennCo Pharmaceuticals. We're one of dozens of nursing homes they use in their geriatric studies. Detective?"

Kevin was already dialing Beth's number as he strode out the door into the frozen sunshine.

THE CONCUSSIVE STRAINS OF HOLST filtered beneath the door to Charles Landon's office, pulsing with crescendos and decrescendos while Beth sat at her desk. Interesting music to make out to, but she wasn't complaining. If she couldn't hear her boss, then he couldn't hear her, either.

With the bright sunshine of the clear winter morning streaming through her window, she didn't need to turn on the lights to see the information popping up on her computer screen. She'd barely taken the time to shrug her parka over the back of her chair before booting up the GlennCo server and logging in.

She knew better than to interrupt her boss while the music was playing in his office. No doubt he and Deborah were "stealing" a little time together. There was still almost half an hour before the building would fill with co-workers and executives running around in a mad, demanding dash before the board meeting this afternoon. Charles and Deborah had probably used the personal elevator that led straight from the parking garage up to the penthouse office. Other than checking in with the guard in the lobby, Beth's presence hadn't even been detected yet.

Which was just the way she'd planned it. She could tune out the music and the activity on the other side of that door. Thirty minutes of Charles Landon gettin' busy with his lovely wife was thirty minutes of uninterrupted time when Beth could plug in the flash drive she'd found in her purse to see if she could access the encrypted files and find out if it was the missing data her boss had been looking for.

If it was, figuring out how and why that data had gotten into her purse was something she'd worry about later.

"Let's see." Even though she'd tried to retrieve the information on her home computer last night—giving up on sleep once she accepted that the taste and heat and power of Kevin Grove's kiss wasn't going to be leaving her memory long enough to let her relax—she hadn't been able to read the files on the memory stick. But running the files on the mother system where they'd been created should improve her chances of success—and appease her curiosity to know what the weirdness of the past forty-eight hours was all about. She scrolled the cursor over the icons on the screen and tried to make sense of the numbers and coded file names. If this was research data, it was in its roughest form—nothing like the summarized documentation she helped Dr. Landon put together. These were most likely the names of different medicinal compounds GlennCo was testing. Beth double clicked on *HE4210*. "Will you open?"

Password Required.

Well, that was more than she'd been able to pull up at home. If she could crack the encryption, she might finally find some answers.

Beth drummed her fingers on top of her desk, thinking of options from the most basic—*Landon*, *Charles*, *Open Sesame*—to something decidedly more complicated—0-1-0 variations, the names of each of Landon's wives, chemical elements—and typing them in. But nothing seemed to unlock the hidden files.

She supposed the easiest thing would be to show Dr. Landon the memory stick, and simply ask him if this was the missing data he'd been looking for. But how would she explain it showing up in her purse when she knew darn well she hadn't put it there? A midnight attack, a man following her and the music of the planets kept her at her desk, busily trying every trick she knew to get the computer files to open.

"Well, hell." Beth heard herself repeating the words she'd heard Kevin growl on more than one occasion, and instantly her mind and body went back to the unexpected passion of the kiss they'd shared last night. The prickly discomfort of all that masculine need flooding her senses, but stopping short of satisfying a purely feminine craving inside her, returned in full force, making the tips of her breasts tingle with longing and her heart squeeze with an unfamiliar ache.

The fact that Kevin Grove could so adamantly deny the attraction between them made her wonder if he might really be the beast her first impression of him had given her. How cruel did a man have to be to set her on fire like that—make her feel like the sexiest, most irresistible woman on the planet—and then tell her she meant nothing to him? Or maybe the beast himself was the one who'd been abused. How badly had *Sheila* and the harassment accusations wounded him so that he no longer recognized or believed that she might like him? The scars that marked Kevin's shoulder and chest must be nothing compared to the damage inside him.

Beth didn't have a lot of experience with men, but she suspected that Kevin had some sort of feelings for her. Whether it was animal lust, a need to be accepted or something more, she couldn't say. For a man who didn't mince words, he certainly was sending her a mixed batch of signals.

"Get over it," she chided herself, moving her fingers over the keyboard and typing in another dozen passwords to no avail.

If Kevin Grove just wanted to be a cop and not get involved with her, then that was his choice. She'd be doing more harm if she forced the issue, right? They could be friends. They had to be neighbors. But she wouldn't let him insult her taste in men or excuse another kiss as pity or gratitude, and intimate that she didn't know her own mind. Let him have his solitude if that's what the big brute wanted. It was her own problem if thoughts of a safe haven or shared passion, courtesy of the cop next door, kept her awake at night.

HE4210 blinked on the screen, awaiting a

password. Maybe the file labels weren't drug names after all. "Are these patient codes?"

Beth had typed up plenty of reports for Dr. Landon. The anonymity of their patients testing drugs and placebos had always been well-guarded. But what if there was a name to go with that code? Could that be the password? The idea couldn't flop worse than anything else she'd tried thus far.

After checking the time on her watch, Beth got up and crossed to the file cabinets lining the north wall, opening the drawer labeled H–I. GlennCo had computerized almost every facet of the company over the past decade. Still, Charles Landon was old-school. It was his habit to print out hard copies of everything he analyzed or wrote. While he kept the most sensitive information locked in his safe, Beth's office and a warehouse room on the third floor of the building housed older records, reports and correspondence. Finding a key word in all that paperwork seemed like a daunting task, but searching for a name beginning with "He" on a file with a "4210" code at least gave her some sense of retaking control over her own life again.

She was thumbing through a stack of

Helgoths and Hendersons when it dawned on her that the music in Dr. Landon's office had looped around to replay the softer orchestral arrangements from the beginning of the CD again. Odd. There was something predictable about pills and age—normally, Dr. Landon's early-morning trysts ended like clockwork before the last song played. But not today. She glanced at her watch. Three minutes to nine. Were Dr. and Mrs. Landon even in there? Had they fallen asleep? What if they'd stayed last night and left the CD running over and over? He could walk into her office right now and find her elbow-deep in old files.

"Good morning, Elisabeth. Why are you in here with the lights out? Is that the flash drive I asked you about?"

Damn. Beth shoved the files back inside the drawer and pushed it shut. She snatched her parka from the back of her chair and hurried over to the door to hang it on the coat rack. She flipped on the overhead switch, filling the room with a fluorescent light that cooled the sunshine's warmth.

Board meeting this afternoon, remember? Her first major appearance at a gathering of all of GlennCo's top-ranking officials. Weeks' worth of preparation and planning for the coming year had come down to today. The votes made this afternoon would determine what direction the company would be taking. It could determine the future of her own job.

And she was poking around in file drawers, futilely searching for a word that would lead her to a clue? She should be knocking on Dr. Landon's door, praying he and his wife were dressed, and making sure he was ready for the big day.

Beth smoothed the blue blouse she wore beneath her charcoal wool pant suit as she sat at her desk to retrieve her planner. The first thing she needed to do was close down her screen and remove the mysterious flash drive. But maybe one more try? Oh, heck. The drive had ended up in her possession, hadn't it? Why not try…*Elisabeth.*

She moved her hand over the mouse and clicked.

"Oh, my God." Her reactions seemed to slow down in direct opposition to the speed with which an endless stream of numbers and formulas and lengthy paragraphs scrolled across her screen. *Test subject. Gehirn 330.*

Without a degree in chemistry, she didn't understand half of what she was reading. And there wasn't time to do more than skim the headers. *Clinical trial 4210. Outcome. Side effects.* "Oh. My. God."

Her phone rang and Beth jumped in her seat.

Real time returned as her pulse thundered in her ears. She reached for the phone on her desk. Clearing her throat, she picked it up. "Good morning. Dr. Landon's office, Elisabeth Rogers speaking."

There was a beat of silence. And another. "I tried to give it to you."

"What?" There was no tone, no strength. The voice was barely discernible. "I'm sorry, but I can't hear you."

She heard a soft rush of wind, like a shallow breath. "They took it from you the first time. I'm sorry."

Recognition drained the blood down to her toes. "Charles?" She glanced over her shoulder at the closed door behind her. "Where are you? What's wrong?"

"Last night…in the crowd…"

Beth glued her eyes to her computer screen, suddenly finding her own breath difficult to catch. "Are you talking about the flash drive? I have it. *You* put it in my bag?"

"If they suspect…" His words faded on a soft groan.

"If who? Dr. Landon, what's going on? I don't know what any of this means." She set down the phone and tried his office door. Locked. Damn. She rattled the knob. Knocked. Why hadn't she thought of this sooner? She raced back to her desk to pull her purse from the bottom drawer and retrieve her building keys. She picked up the phone and tried to get some answers. "Charles, where are you? Are you all right?" She strained to hear him over the faint echo of music. Music? "Are you in your office?"

"Too late…" He wheezed out a breath. "…make it right."

"What?" Was that an order to her? Was *he* trying to make something right? The keys were in her fist now. "I don't understand."

Click.

"Dr. Landon?" Silence. "Charles?"

The GlennCo logo floated across her computer monitor as the screensaver kicked in. What the hell did any of this mean? And she'd thought the slower, more predictable life on the farm had been too boring for her.

She was still holding the receiver when her phone rang again. With a startled yelp, she dropped it onto her desk.

Just as quickly, she slapped her hand over her mouth to stifle her panic. *Stop it. Don't be stupid. Think.*

She forced herself to take a deep breath. To clear her head. To hang up.

Different phone. The ringing was coming from her purse. A personal call. While Beth sorted through keys to unlock Dr. Landon's office, she pulled her cell phone from her purse.

If this was something creepy... "Hello?"

"Beth? It's Kevin. Detective Grove," he added unnecessarily. His deep voice was clear and recognizable, impossible to mistake for anyone else's. Her breath rushed out on an embarrassing sigh of relief. But the moment's reprieve from panic didn't last. "I need to talk to you about GlennCo Pharmaceuticals Alzheimer's research. Do you have any free time today?"

"No, today isn't good." She closed the file on her screen and sent it back to the flash drive. Biting down on the urge to tell him about Dr. Landon's cryptic call, she found the right key and unlocked the inner office door. She was tired of turning to Kevin with stories that made no sense. Maybe he didn't have a problem with relationships after all. Maybe it was just the idea of being attracted to a crazy lady that made him wary about things getting personal between them. "There's too much going on at work."

"Is something wrong?"

She pulled the elusive data drive from her computer and tucked it into the pocket of her slacks. "I'm just not having a good start to my d—"

The outside office door banged open and Geneva Landon swept into the room. "Where's Charles?" Her dark red power suit complemented her silvery-white bun and hugged a tall, buxom figure that she used to her advantage as she advanced on Beth. "He hasn't answered my calls. He was supposed to meet me for breakfast at seven. I won't tolerate being stood up like this."

"Beth?"

The phone in her hand was momentarily forgotten as Beth planted herself in Geneva's path. "A breakfast meeting wasn't on his calendar."

"This was personal." The older woman pushed past her.

"Wait." Beth was no lightweight herself. And she was quicker. She reached the door first and grabbed the knob. "You can't go in there."

The older woman pulled back a step and smiled. "I know all about his secret liaisons with Deborah. She's not the first wife he ignored at night and made it up to in the morning."

Beth cringed. Too much information. "Yes, ma'am. Still, I think something's wrong…ow. Hey!" Geneva Landon wasn't a woman accustomed to hearing no. With a lucky bump against Beth's bruised shoulder, she nudged her aside and turned the door knob. Unless Beth resorted to tackling, the woman was gone. She lifted the phone to her ear and apologized. "Kevin, I'm going to have to call you back."

And that's when Geneva screamed.

"Beth!" he shouted.

But she was already hanging up. She dashed into the office behind Geneva Landon, stopping in her tracks as she saw the older woman circle around the big mahogany desk.

She *was* going crazy. Her boss, Charles Landon, sat in his chair, slumped over his blotter, an empty pill bottle clutched in his hand.

"Charles? Charles!" Geneva snapped the order as she pressed her fingers to the side of Dr. Landon's neck. With a shake of her head, she pried the pill bottle from his hands and read the prescription. The orchestra crescendoed in dramatic contrast to the pall of death filling the room. "Call security."

"What about 9-1-1? The police?"

Beth rushed around the desk to help Geneva pull Charles to the floor. She unbuttoned his collar and pulled off his tie while the silver-haired woman put her ear against his chest to listen for a heartbeat. Then she was up on her knees, administering CPR.

"Fine. Call an ambulance. But no police." She stopped to listen for a heartbeat again, and then resumed compressions. Beth thought she detected more anger than concern in the other woman's finely lined features. "He decides to kick off on the day of GlennCo's board meeting and the votes that have to be cast regarding the company's future? I was counting on you, Charles."

Geneva raised her head, her dark gaze boring holes into Beth's eyes. "We handle this internally. Go. And kill that damn music."

Chapter Seven

A lamb among the lions.

That was Kevin's first impression of Beth Rogers, sitting on the leather couch, arms hugged around her middle, tears drying on her cheeks, while she dutifully answered Atticus Kincaid's questions. The rest of the players in the room either hovered around her or kept their eye on her from across the room. They were so focused on Beth that they hadn't yet picked up on his bulk lurking outside the entrance to Charles Landon's office.

But she did.

Those soft gray-blue eyes locked on to his.

It'll be okay, lady, he wanted to say. But then, he didn't make promises he wasn't sure he could keep.

No promises was the message she must

have read on his face because she blinked and looked away. She tucked a wisp of mink-colored hair behind her ear and sat up a little straighter, rallying her own strength to answer the next question.

Right. One of them needed to keep things professional and distant between them. Charging across town and calling in favors didn't exactly speak to his ability to deper-sonalize his feelings for Beth Rogers.

His *think like a cop* mantra warred with Miriam's *"Is Beth important to you?"* advice.

Yeah. The woman was important, he admitted. More than she should be with what he knew about relationships. But that didn't mean Beth Rogers couldn't use a cop on her side right about now. *Think like a cop.*

While the injustice of the mismatch between executives and one lone assistant simmered in his veins, Kevin took a moment to assess the big shots of GlennCo Pharmaceuticals whom the guard at the front desk had listed for him. The big boss, Raymond Glenn, was easy to spot—rimless glasses, designer suit, air of entitlement. The silver-haired woman in the blood-red suit was Geneva Landon, the deceased's first wife. She was stoic as she stood with her arm around a weeping blonde. Mid-twenties, big diamond on her left hand—he was guessing the current Mrs. Landon. Now that was an odd alliance. There were others in the room, as well, far too many to keep from contaminating the crime scene if, indeed, that was what this tragedy proved to be.

Oh, yeah. And not one of them was happy about having the police here. But he wasn't about to let Beth's harried responses to his call this morning—or a woman's scream—go unexplained. And once the 9-1-1 call for a bus came over the wire… A quick call to Atticus at KCPD headquarters, only a few blocks from the Kansas City high-rise housing GlennCo's American offices, put someone he trusted on the scene thirty minutes before Kevin could speed through morning traffic and get here himself.

The EMTs who'd responded to the call had already covered the body on the floor behind the desk and were packing their gear. Another guard, whose uniform matched the man's at the lobby desk, stood over them, following their movements as much as he was protecting the dead body.

In a rarity Kevin was unaccustomed to, but refused to be intimidated by, a dark-haired man who matched him in height and brawn excused himself from his position beside Atticus and moved to block Kevin's entrance. "I'm Tyler James, GlennCo's chief of security. This area is restricted."

In what sense of the word?

Taking note of the holster bulge beneath the security chief's blazer, Kevin opened his coat and flashed the badge hanging from around his neck. "Kevin Grove. KCPD. Back off, James."

With a grunt of displeasure, James stepped aside to let Kevin enter the plush office, but he had no intention of leaving his side. "This isn't a police matter. From everything I've seen, it looks like Dr. Landon killed himself with an overdose of his heart medication and, uh, you know, those male enhancement pills. A doctor would know better than to take that combination by accident."

Kevin spotted only one empty pill bottle on the desk. A lethal combination would require two. "We'll let the M.E. decide that."

"Look, I'm happy to cooperate in any way I can." James touched Kevin's coat sleeve, demanding his full attention as he leaned in to whisper. "But we don't want to panic our investors. For the company's interests, we're trying to keep news of a board member's suicide contained."

"Then don't talk to anybody but me or my partner."

He walked away from the curse stuttering over Tyler James's lips and met Atticus beside the victim's body. He knelt down to uncover Charles Landon's pale, pinched expression, noting that he seemed to have died in pain—or under protest—before pulling the plastic blanket back over Landon's face and standing. "Anything here look funny to you?"

"Besides the standing-room-only crowd?" Atticus handed him a sheet of GlennCo stationery in a clear plastic bag. "Here's the alleged suicide note. Neatly typed on a computer. Apparently, the brand of printer on his desk is standard issue throughout the building."

I'm sorry. It's my fault. I let the company down.

Love to my wife.

Charles.

Kevin read the note and handed it back to Atticus. "No signature to verify he wrote it."

"The EMTs said Landon was already on the floor when they arrived. They tried to re-suscitate him, but he was dead when they got here. Your friend Beth said she and the older Mrs. Landon found him slumped over his desk."

That would explain the scream that had sent Kevin running across the Oak Park nursing home lot to his SUV. "I take it they tried to revive him, too?"

Atticus nodded. "Lots of hands on this body. Holly, my sister-in-law, is on her way to claim the vic and give us a T.O.D. as well as a preliminary cause of death. But I don't know how much usable evidence we'll find around here."

"Keep me posted." Kevin paused before he turned away. "And thanks, A. I know we've already got two homicides on our plate—"

"I said all you had to do was call." With a nod of his dark head, Atticus went back to jotting observations in his notebook.

Inevitably, Kevin's attention shifted back

to Beth. She was on her feet now, but cornered. Raymond Glenn might have lowered his voice to a whisper, but there was no doubt that the CEO was grilling her. "You were right on the other side of that door. And you didn't hear anything?"

"From the first day I started here, Charles told me never to interrupt him while the music was playing. I thought Deborah was with him." She squeezed her eyes shut, stemming the pool of tears gathering there. She opened them again, a flash of fire sparking in their depths. "I didn't know he was in here dying. Believe me, I would have called for help."

"Sounds to me like Charles did. But you didn't answer."

Raymond Glenn's veiled accusation was enough to rile Kevin. Screw this keep-his-distance crap. He reached around the gray-haired man and grabbed Beth's hand, pulling her to his side. "If you don't mind, my partner and I will ask the questions." Tightening his grip around the chilled flex of her fingers, Kevin raised his voice and made an announcement to the entire room. "I need you all to wait outside until we're ready to take your statements. Mr. James? You want to help? Find an empty office to escort these people to, and keep them contained until we're ready for them."

"No! I want to stay with my husband." Deborah Landon broke free of Geneva's hold and dashed across the room.

But Atticus was there to stop her from touching anything. "Ma'am, I'm sorry. You'll have to go with the others for now."

Tyler James broke away from the reluctant exodus and tucked the distraught widow beneath his arm. "Deborah. Come with me. I promise we'll take good care of him."

Atticus pointed to the door. "You have to leave, too, James. This is our crime scene now."

With a defiant tilt of his chin, the security chief pulled Deborah Landon toward the door. "There's no crime here. Just a tragic loss for the company. And Mrs. Landon here, of course."

Atticus didn't so much as bat an eye. "We'll see."

Deborah Landon paused to blow her late husband a kiss. "Bye, Charlie. I love you."

Once the room had emptied of GlennCo personnel, Kevin turned to his partner. "You okay here?"

Atticus slipped his knowing, gray-eyed gaze to Beth before nodding and going back to work. "I've got this covered."

While Atticus stayed with the body and EMTs to catalogue items in the room, Kevin took Beth out to her office and closed the door behind them. He could feel the tremors in her hand, but it might be from anger as much as fear. He wasn't ready to let go when she pulled away and headed for the opposite door. "I suppose you want me to wait across the hall with the others."

When she started to open the door, Kevin's palm was there to shut it. He stayed where he was, his chest nearly touching her back, his arm stretched above her shoulder, his nose breathing in the enticing scents of vanilla and spice that clung to her hair. Hell. Maybe *he* was the one shaking.

"You okay?" he asked.

She curled her fingers into fists and rested her forehead against the door, working through a silent sob. "I just lost a mentor. And a friend." Her fingers splayed open again, her hand looking delicate and pale beside his. "They think I called the police. I can feel it every time they look at me. Like I'm some kind of traitor."

Kevin resisted the urge to slide his hand over hers, but couldn't find the will to retreat. "Am I making this worse? Do you want Atticus and me to leave?"

Her shoulders trembled as she turned and flattened her back against the door. She fingered the opening of his coat, touched the badge hanging there. And then she tilted those sweet blue eyes up to his and tried to smile. "No."

Good. Dangerous, perhaps. But good.

"If this is ruled a suicide, it won't fall under KCPD jurisdiction and I can't help you."

"It wasn't suicide."

"Accidental death, then. A man dies of a heart attack, you call the coroner, not the cops."

Her hands found their way inside his coat to straighten the knot of his tie. "I think he was murdered."

Kevin captured both her hands with one of his and stilled their constant motion by holding them tight against his chest. "Did you tell any of them that?"

She shrugged. "I don't have proof. Just a feeling. But I know he didn't kill himself. He took meticulous care of his health. Loved his grandchildren. He'd scheduled a Christmas vacation with Deborah. A man who plans ahead like that doesn't commit suicide. And that note to his wife? He would have signed it 'Charlie,' not 'Charles.' You heard her. That's what she always called him."

"That's not a lot to base an assumption of murder on."

When her gaze dropped to their hands, he eased his grip. But she didn't pull away. "He was on the phone with me when he died. I didn't piece it together in time, but I must have heard his very last words."

"Which were?"

She tilted her face back up to his. "'Make it right.' I think he's the one who put that flash drive in my purse. I think it's the missing research data. He was trying to tell me something—something he couldn't come right out and say. I got the files to open, but I couldn't make much sense of them. Yet."

Kevin nodded, releasing her to smooth the dark brown bangs away from her eyes. "Okay."

"Okay, what?"

"I'm on the case."

Her hands fisted in his jacket, catching a

bit of shirt and skin underneath. "You believe me?"

He didn't mind the little pinch one bit. That little tug on his skin made him feel alive. Connected. Call him twenty kinds of fool, but he was in this mess for as long as Beth needed him. "You are either the best actress I've ever met—and trust me, I've already met the best—or you, lady, have stumbled onto something you shouldn't have."

"You don't think I'm crazy?"

"Nah." Kevin brushed the velvety wisps of her hair off her cheek before tunneling his fingers into the soft thickness at her nape. He dipped his mouth and grazed his lips over the purple mark bruising her cheek. He pressed another kiss to her forehead.

He paused at her mouth, giving her the chance to push him away.

She didn't.

Kevin claimed what she offered.

"I believe you."

"To our friend and colleague, Charles Landon. We'll miss you."

Beth raised her glass in a toast along with Raymond Glenn and the board members and staff gathered around the table in the GlennCo headquarters conference room. But she set the potent alcohol down without taking a drink that might cloud her mind or give any credence to this travesty of an impromptu memorial service. By the time Mr. Glenn had locked up his bottle of bourbon in the liquor cabinet at the end of the room and tossed his keys into the drawer on top, Beth had taken her place by the windows and opened her laptop to take notes the way she had for Dr. Landon at similar meetings.

After a quick introduction of the twelve board members seated around the table, Mr. Glenn welcomed the blond woman seated in Dr. Landon's chair. "Deborah, you *are* allowed to vote in Charles's place, according to company bylaws."

Even though the agenda had been significantly curtailed, Raymond Glenn had insisted on convening the GlennCo board of directors meeting that afternoon. Beth sat in her corner chair behind the spot where Charles had once sat, typing notes onto her laptop. Other than Deborah's presence, and the puffy red eyes of several board members around the room, it was being run like any other meeting.

Raymond commanded the room from his spot at the head of the long conference table. "We owe it to our investors to have a clear plan of action for the new year. With this tight economy, they're looking for financial security. The board's indecision won't give them that."

"Shouldn't we table these discussions at least for a few days?" Deborah asked, her voice croaky with grief. "I haven't even made funeral arrangements."

"I apologize for being the tough guy here. But some hard decisions have to be made for next year. The motion is on the table to move forward with our production of Gehirn 330. Geneva, is the promotional campaign in place and ready to launch?"

Even the Iron Butterfly of the boardroom had been rattled by her former husband's death, it seemed. She took a moment to compose herself before answering. "I want to run it by a trial audience first, but—"

Beth interrupted. This was wrong. This was all just wrong. "Dr. Landon was against the production of Gehirn 330."

All eyes in the room snapped to her corner by the windows. Geneva Landon groused. "You don't have the floor—"

"Did he tell you that?" asked Silas Ramsey, the elderly board member sitting beside her.

Beth figuratively stood her ground. "I know he wanted to look at Dr. Allen's data again."

Glenn shoved a thick printout into the center of the conference table. "I have all of Dr. Allen's research right here in Charles's report. According to the lab, the clinical trials were a success. All the necessary modifications for product safety have been made. Side effects are minimal. The drug works."

Geneva passed the binder to Silas, who passed it on to Deborah, who heaved it over her shoulder with an impatient sigh into Beth's hands. A quick thumb through the pages revealed information just as confusing and complicated as the scientific data on the flash drive still burning a hole of guilt in the pocket of her slacks. How was she going to make sense of any of this? How was she supposed to help Charles if she didn't know what he'd wanted her to do with the data?

Raymond Glenn had risen and was now circling the table. If this was a courtroom, he'd be the prosecutor giving his final summation. "Of course, I would have liked to have had Charles give us the thumbs-up in person in his presentation, but I think his stamp of approval on this report—" he paused beside Beth to pick up the binder "—gives us the go-ahead to put Gehirn 330 on the market. We can change lives because of Charles's vision, give him a fitting tribute by reversing the onset of Alzheimer's."

Deborah Landon raised her hand. "Could you name the new medicine after Charlie?"

Raymond nodded. "Good idea." He set the binder at the head of the table again, and pointed to Geneva. "Can your team brainstorm some product names? Or work Charles's name prominently into the documentation?"

Geneva smoothed her flawless hair, trying to mask the stunned expression on her face. "We already have three different promotion campaigns in place, ready for consumer testing. Nothing against dear Charles, but coming up with something new at this point would cause expensive delays."

"Expensive I can absorb. Delays I won't stand for. Do what you can." Leaving Geneva Landon's open-mouthed protest unanswered, he sat. "Anything else for the good of the order?"

A dispirited chorus of "no"s triggered a general shuffle of movement around the table, as board members, staff and guests gathered their things in preparation for adjournment.

"Well, I do have a couple more things." Raymond's sober announcement stopped all activity. "One, Charles was my business partner for many years. We started this company together. We took GlennCo public and built it into a world leader. Long before that, he was my friend." He paused to swallow the emotion choking his throat. "Over the next couple of weeks, take whatever time you need to mourn our loss. Be with your families. Celebrate the holidays. Starting tomorrow, we'll function with a skeleton staff for now and get back to work after the New Year—maybe just enough people to answer phones and field questions from the press for now. And finally—" his dark gaze settled on Deborah, then glanced around the table before stopping at Beth "—I want to make GlennCo security available to any of you who are…upset…by Charles's death." He looked to the security chief standing with his arms crossed near the room's double doors. "Tyler, can you arrange that?"

"Yes, sir." The big man nodded. "We can walk you to your cars, screen clients who enter the building, run security checks on anyone you deem suspicious."

"Wouldn't counselors make more sense than beefed-up security?" Beth dared to ask. "Or don't you think Dr. Landon's death was a suicide?"

"I think…I need to do a better job of taking care of the people who are important to me. I wish now that I'd done a better job of taking care of Charles. He must have been calling for help and none of us realized it." He crossed the length of the room and lay a hand on her shoulder. "Look at you, Miss Rogers. Mugged in your own home and now this. I should be protecting you instead of just passing you by in the break room. You're a valuable employee to the company. You are all valuable to me," he insisted, finally moving away. "Prayers and comfort to you all. And Deborah? Let us know if there's anything we can do." Raymond Glenn resumed his seat at the head of the table. The company-as-family moment had passed. It was back to business. "So, are we making millions with Gehirn 330? How does everyone vote?"

"I DON'T NEED YOU TO DRIVE me home, Mr. James," Beth said to the beefy man who'd bumped into her at the lobby security desk. After checking out, she set her purse on the counter for the guard to inspect while she zipped up her parka and wrapped her scarf around her neck. "I'm perfectly fine. Besides, I'd be stuck at home in the morning without a way to get to work."

"I could pick you up, as well," he offered.

Um, no. His sudden buddy-buddy behavior, coupled with a striking resemblance to the large build of the man who'd attacked her and followed her into the Plaza parking garage, made the offer more unsettling than comforting.

Beth grabbed her purse and slung it over her shoulder, anxious to get back to the relative safety and familiarity of her own home before either Tyler or the guard decided to search her person. If the guilt she felt at carrying the potentially incriminating flash drive in her pocket didn't show on her face, it was certainly branding her deeper inside.

"Don't be silly." She smiled, waving aside his offer. "I'm heading straight home. My Jeep's in perfect working order and besides, I enjoy the commute. I think I can use the quiet time alone today, especially."

"Understandable," he conceded. He reached across the counter and typed his logout code into the computer. "At least let me walk you to your car. I'm heading to the garage anyway."

"That isn't nec—"

"Come on." He picked up his long coat from the counter and shrugged it on, giving her a clear glimpse of the gun beneath his left arm and the security badge he wore. "The boss is riding my case about the welfare of his employees. I think he's especially worried that, with the cops showing up, and you finding the body—"

"Actually, Geneva did."

"—that you might be too upset to drive on your own."

"I'm a grown-up, Mr. James. I appreciate your concern, but I've dealt with death before."

"Let me do my job, ma'am." He touched her elbow and turned her toward the parking garage exit. "I'll walk you to your car, follow you home—then I can call Mr. Glenn and assure him everything's hunky dory and be on my way." Beth shifted away from his light grip, but he slowed his stride to keep pace beside her. "You can't tell me you're not rattled by Dr. Landon's death."

She couldn't. Maybe Kevin Grove wasn't the only big man whose intentions she'd misjudged. *Big* didn't make Tyler James her attacker any more than it did Kevin, though his solicitous attention this evening made her decidedly uncomfortable. And would raising too much of a stink about GlennCo's newfound concern for her well-being make Tyler suspicious of *her?* There were other coworkers filing out to their cars in the garage. As long as she wasn't alone with him, that was caution enough, yes? "Okay. Walk me to my car. I'll take it from there."

Beth was driving down Highway 24, coming up on the turn into her neighborhood, before she realized his friendly good-night and wave didn't mean Tyler James had agreed to her compromise. She hadn't spotted him in the bumper-to-bumper traffic getting out of downtown. She must have left him in the dust on Interstate 70. But there was no mistaking the hulking shadow behind the wheel of the dark car that made the turn right after her.

There was no mistaking the frissons of fear and suspicion twisting in her stomach, either. Maybe she'd been too quick to judge Tyler James—as innocent. Why was the man following her?

She released the steering wheel to touch her hip, where the flash drive was still hidden beneath layers of clothing. Did he suspect she had this? Did Mr. Glenn? Who besides Charles Landon knew it existed? And just what did it contain that warranted assault and subterfuge and murder? Because she was having fewer and fewer doubts that Dr. Landon's odd behavior and the events that followed were all connected in some sinister fashion.

With a sinking heart, Beth noticed the porch light was on at Kevin's house—a definite sign that no one was home. But Hank Whitaker was outside, chipping away at the ice that had formed at the end of his driveway. Beth made a point of honking and waving until the older gentleman looked up from his work and saluted her.

Witnesses meant safety, right? She ignored the habit of pressing her garage-door opener as she approached her house and parked in the driveway. Tyler's dark green car pulled up to the curb behind her. She was out of the Jeep, storming toward him as soon as he climbed out of his car.

"Why are you following me when I specifically asked you not to? You didn't trail any other employees to their homes. What makes me so special?"

"Ease up, sweetheart. You're the only one who was attacked." Tyler halted at the edge of her driveway, his leather gloved hands raised in placating surrender. "We think it may have been Dr. Landon who went after you."

"Charles?" No way.

"Surely you noticed he hadn't been himself lately. If he was up to something that didn't pan out, he was obsessed with you, or he just had a screw loose—any of those are reason enough for a man to feel shame and kill himself." His expression softened with pity. "Do you know how many of his wives used to be his assistant?"

Let me guess. "Four?"

"He may have been targeting you as number five."

Beth pressed a hand to her temple and shook her head. "No. Dr. Landon was a mentor. A father figure." *A man in some kind of trouble.* He'd reached out to her for help and she hadn't even known it. Now he was dead. And she couldn't believe it had been his choice. "He never would have hurt me."

"Yeah, well, that kind of misplaced loyalty is why Mr. Glenn is worried about your state of mind tonight."

"My state of mind? So siccing you on me is supposed to be some kind of comfort?"

He dropped his hands. His patient expression hardened. "Ma'am, you're blowing this all out of proportion. I'm just here to make sure there's no more fallout after what happened today. Mr. Glenn is worried about bad publicity for the company."

So his *concern* wasn't about her at all. "Maybe he should be. Insisting on that meeting this afternoon when all of us are grieving? Just so he could get his precious new drug into production?"

"He's thinking about our future when some of us aren't thinking very clearly at all."

He didn't have to point a finger to know he was referring to her. "Get off my property."

"Look, Elisabeth—most of us have family. Deborah Landon has a live-in maid. But we know you live alone. You heard Mr. Glenn today. He wants to take better care of—"

A thunderous bark from the sidewalk gave Beth a heads-up only a moment before a brindle-colored torpedo launched itself at them. "Daisy?"

"What the hell? Look out!" Tyler jumped aside as Beth took the full force of massive paws in the middle of her stomach, sprawling her on her fanny in the snow.

The icy shock of wet and cold seeping through her clothes gave way to a moment of panic as the dog's square jaw with drool frozen in its wrinkles cocked her head to one side and barked at her again. Beth put her hands over her ears and tried to slither her way backward through the snow, but a deep-pitched voice commanded Daisy to sit—on Beth's legs—anchoring her to the spot.

"Good girl." When Kevin Grove jogged up in a gray KCPD sweatshirt and black knit watch cap, he snatched up the leash trailing behind the panting mastiff mix and reached out a gloved hand to help Beth to her feet. "She just wants to get to know you." Reassurance aside, while Beth brushed the snow off her slacks, Kevin faced off against Tyler James. "Beth's not alone."

"Grove." He pulled his hand from the holster beneath his arm and buttoned his coat. "Isn't this a surprise."

"You weren't going to shoot my dog, were you?"

"It's my job to protect GlennCo employees. I thought he was attacking her."

"*She* was just greeting Beth with an enthusiastic hello." Kevin spared a glance over his shoulder to Beth without ever really taking his focus off the GlennCo security chief. "Is there a problem?"

"No problem."

"Yes," she answered at the same time. "He followed me home and he won't leave."

"Now who am I inclined to believe?"

Tyler looked from Kevin's steely glare down to Beth. "I'm just carrying out my orders to look after you. See you home. Check out the house. Are you sure you want this guy and that…thing here?"

Daisy woofed as the glove pointed her way. Tyler quickly snatched his hand back.

Beth linked her arm through Kevin's and bravely laid her hand on Daisy's broad head. The big dog saw the touch as a friendly invitation and pushed herself into Beth's surprisingly willing caress. "Yes, I do. Thank Mr. Glenn for his concern—and for yours. But I'll be just fine. I'll see you in the morning at work."

Leaving a scowling Tyler behind in her driveway, Beth escorted Kevin up to her front door and unlocked the house. He hesitated a moment on the porch, pulling back on Daisy's leash. But Beth clicked her tongue behind her teeth. "C'mon, girl." Daisy bounded in after her, leaving Kevin little choice but to follow them both inside. He closed the door and bolted it behind him.

Beth had grown up with dogs, though admittedly none the size of a small pony, and found herself breathing a sigh of relief at the normalcy of Daisy sniffing her way from chair to sofa to dining room table, familiarizing herself with the smells of the house.

"When she thaws out, she'll leave a mess on your carpet," Kevin apologized.

Wet dog she could deal with. "I don't mind. Her timing was impeccable. Now that I'm learning she's all bark and no bite, I think I'm going to like Daisy."

"So. What's for dinner?"

"Excuse me?" She turned to see Kevin at her front window, peeking through the blinds. Did he always run the dog with a gun strapped to his back? Had he been expecting some kind of trouble?

She quickly shifted her gaze to his eyes as he turned. "You said you were going to cook me something as a thank-you." He thumbed over his shoulder out the window. "I introduced myself to Hank across the street. He promised to keep an eye on things when I can't be here. But my shift is over. Daisy and I got our two miles in. I'm thinking I'm hungry."

"He's still outside, isn't he?" Beth hurried over to the window. Kevin's arm went out like a barricade, preventing her from getting right up to the blinds to look for herself. But she still caught a glance of the dark green car parked on the street out front. She latched on to the protective forearm and sank back onto her heels. "Can't the man take a hint? Do you think he knows Charles's death wasn't a suicide? Do they suspect me?"

"Possibly. You were the only one in that office this morning."

"His wife Deborah must have been there. The music was playing when I arrived."

"Music?"

"Classical stuff. It's a high sign to warn me—and to mask any sounds—when they're in there making out."

"But you didn't see her?"

Beth thought back to the chaos of the morning, from sneaking in early to Kevin's last, caring kiss. "They come and go by Dr. Landon's private elevator. I don't know if it's discretion as much as they think it's fun to sneak around." The images began to pop into place. "But, no. She wasn't there when Geneva barged in and found him. And I went in right after her. I remember Deborah being there after your partner, Atticus, arrived—Geneva called her on her cell phone. But I never saw her before that. I just assumed they'd had their tête-à-tête and she'd gone."

"Did anyone see *you?*"

"I…" Beth suddenly pictured what sneaking into the office before hours, leaving the lights off and trying to crack security codes must look like to a seasoned detective like Kevin. "I didn't kill him."

"I know. But suicide or murder, you were on the scene and you had the opportunity to be involved with his death. If James is any good at his job, and I think he might be, he wants to find out what you know." Kevin unzipped her parka and pushed the bright blue nylon off her shoulders. When she thought he might pull her into his arms for another of those hold-on-for-the-ride kisses, he instead stuffed her coat into her arms and turned back to the window. Guarding her. "He's on the phone—either reporting in that you got home safe and sound like he said— or telling someone he couldn't get inside to scope out your place or interview you."

"You're not leaving until he does, right?" The answer was written there in the intensity of the golden brown eyes that met hers. He'd keep her safe, even if they weren't quite sure what the danger was or where it was coming from. Beth smiled, tossed her coat over the back of a dining-room chair and headed into the kitchen. "How do hamburgers sound?"

"Better than what I had planned. You have

an old towel I can dry off Daisy's paws with? Sorry about the take-down. Once she gets going, she has a hard time putting on the brakes."

Several hours later, with her French doors repaired, their plates clean and Daisy appeased with a hamburger of her own and a blanket draped over the couch to sleep on, Beth rolled over in her own bed. The dark of the winter night had found its way beneath the covers to chill her through her flannel pajama pants and long-sleeved T-shirt. Or maybe it was the fear and confusion lurking at the corners of her mind that was chilling her from the inside out.

Normally when she couldn't sleep, Beth got up and worked on something mundane that would bore her into drowsy relaxation again. There was wallpaper to scrape in the main bathroom, bills to pay. She threw back the covers and climbed out of bed, stopping in her bedroom doorway and looking across the hallway into her office. The red power button on her computer glowed in the shadows, and for a few moments, she thought about running the flash drive again, to see if she could read it on her home computer, now that she knew at least one password. But the soft lamp light shining from her living room drew her down the hallway on silent, stockinged feet.

Kevin looked up from the book he was reading as soon as she appeared at the end of the hall. He peered over the top of a pair of reading glasses that gave his craggy features an intellectual appeal. "It's late."

Daisy lifted her drowsy head to acknowledge Beth's presence before snugging her nose back against Kevin's thigh and snorting with fatigue.

Rubbing her hands up and down her arms, trying to hold on to some kind of warmth, Beth stepped into the dim circle of light. She didn't know if the gun resting on the end table beside her two guests should reassure her or frighten her. "He's gone, isn't he?"

"Yeah. About two hours ago."

But Tyler James had watched the house all through dinner. He'd made another call from his car when Kevin had gone back to his house to change into jeans and return with the tools and wood to repair her French doors.

Beth made herself say the polite thing.

"You don't have to stay." Although having the extra bodies around, with the heat and sense of security they provided, went a long way toward easing the isolation she felt.

"It's easier to watch over you from here. I'm running some background checks and waiting for the M.E.'s autopsy results, so there's nothing more I can follow up on tonight. I'd be awake over at my house, watching through the window, worrying I was too far away to help if something else happened to you." Kevin pulled off his glasses. "Unless you want me to leave."

She shook her head.

"You should go back to bed."

"I can't sleep."

He held up the book. "Neither can I. And I'm dead tired." He set the book and glasses on the table, next to his holstered weapon and gave the dog a shove. "Daisy, move."

"She's okay." Beth sat at the far end of the sofa with the length of the dog between them. She curled her legs up beneath her as she adjusted her position to stroke Daisy's warm, mottled flank. "What happened to her? Why does her skin look like this—all patchwork with fur and scars?"

"Neglect." Kevin stretched his arm across the back of the sofa. "She was left outside a drug house—they didn't take into account that she was more couch potato than guard dog. She was just a decoration to them, I guess—not a living, feeling creature. She nearly starved. She contracted mange and then instead of taking her to a vet, they tried to treat her with some chemical that burned parts of her skin."

"That sounds awful. It's a wonder she's still such a gentle—albeit loud and kind of clumsy—giant."

"My friend Liza's a veterinarian at a shelter downtown. She got Daisy's skin healthy again, fattened her up. But with three dogs and a husband at her house already, they just didn't have space and were looking for a home for her." Daisy licked her jowls with contentment. "I figured we were a good match."

So Daisy had a big heart, too, that belied her fierce-looking exterior. If only someone cared enough to see it. "You rescued her?"

"One of Liza's rescue dogs saved my life once. I figured I'd return the favor by paying it forward. Nobody wanted her."

"You did."

"She's why I bought the house and moved out of my apartment." He dropped his hand to scratch behind the dog's ears. "You never know what you'll do for a woman you care about, I guess."

Beth's hand stilled on Daisy's thigh as some unnamed emotion constricted her heart. Was she supposed to read anything into that comment? Or was he strictly talking dogs and old girlfriends? Beth couldn't figure out her feelings for Kevin Grove any better than she understood why she'd been given a flash drive filled with incomprehensible codes and a man she'd cared about had died.

Beth pulled her sleeves down to her knuckles and tucked her arms around her waist again, fighting off a shiver. "Why are these things happening to me?"

Kevin scraped his palm over the golden stubble shading his jaw and shook his head. "I don't know the answers to that yet."

"I feel like my world is spinning out of control. Like I can't hold on to anything that makes sense."

His eyes darkened to the color of fine

whiskey as his gaze locked onto hers. And then, despite her protests and the dog's, as well, he was shoving Daisy to the floor and tossing the blanket after her.

"Come here." Kevin reached for Beth, pulled her into his arms, settled her in his lap. His thighs burned into her bottom. His scent surrounded her. He flattened her palm against the soft cotton of his sweatshirt and encouraged her to latch onto the harder muscle underneath. "I'm solid. Do you feel that?" She nodded against the strong beat of his heart, snuggling close as his arms folded tight around her. "You hold on to me. I'm not going anywhere."

"Promise?"

"Yeah." For a man who didn't mince words, it was promise enough.

In a matter of minutes, Beth fell into the warmest, most exhausted, most secure sleep of her life.

Chapter Eight

Kevin woke up on fire.

The house was still save for Daisy's deep snore. The morning outside the front windows was still dark. His neck was a little cramped from sleeping on a couch that was too short for his frame, but that hitch of pain quickly receded as his body awoke to one feverish sensation after another.

Warm spice and vanilla teased his nose. Dark, velvety hair caught in the morning stubble on his chin. Sometime during the night he'd pulled off his sweatshirt, leaving nothing but a thin layer of cotton between his bare chest and the twin pearls at the tips of pillowed breasts branding his skin. Long legs tangled with his. A soft palm claimed the swell of his pectoral muscle and the turgid male nipple standing at attention beneath it.

His hands were full of sweet, sassy curves as his waking mind identified the possessive grip he had on Beth's bottom and the warm skin at the nip of her waist.

He was aroused. He was wanting. And he was painfully aware that the fierce need coursing through his veins was not what Beth had had in mind when she'd come to him looking for companionship and comfort last night.

How did he wriggle his way out of this one without embarrassing her? And why the hell wasn't he making any effort to move away from the intimate cloak of her body?

"You awake?"

Well, hell. She knew?

Beth tipped her chin up and rested it on her fist atop his chest to look him straight in the eye. "I'm still holding on."

Kevin's breath caught in his chest as he lost his thoughts in the depths of her gray-blue eyes. He shouldn't do this. He was here to protect her. She might be the key to solving a murder, to uncovering a conspiracy at GlennCo. The last time he'd tried to keep a woman safe, it had nearly cost him his job. It had damn well cost him his faith in everything he wanted from Beth right now.

He let himself reach up and brush the hair from her cheek. He touched the butterfly bandages that protected the stitches at her hairline. But then he saw that his hand was shaking and he curled his fingers into a fist. Was he that needy? That starved for affection? That…in love with Elisabeth Rogers?

"Is Beth important to you?"

Sucker. He was so gonna be screwed by the time this was all over and she was out of his life.

"Lady, I can't…" His voice was little more than a husky growl in his throat.

She pressed a finger over his lips. "It's okay. I want you, too."

He shook his head. She didn't understand how out of practice he was. She couldn't imagine the kind of longing a lonesome beast like him kept locked inside. He lifted her hips and tried to move to a less obvious position beneath her, but when he set her back down, her legs split on either side of his thigh and she clenched around him—just the way he wanted to feel her squeeze around…

"Kev?" Her soft little gasp danced across every nerve in his body like a firm caress.

"Ah, hell." Kevin tipped his head back against the arm rest and groaned in agony, locking every muscle into place, willing his body not to react. "It won't be the way you think. I'm a little past patient seduction, and I don't have much finesse to begin with."

"Then just do it." She rubbed her palms over his short hair and cupped the back of his head, forcing him to look into those irresistibly expressive eyes again. "I need to feel something besides fear. I want to be certain of something in my life. And I *know* we want each other." She rode the ragged rise and fall of his chest. "I want to feel desire. Passion. I want—"

He stopped up her words with a kiss, forcing her soft lips to part, thrusting his tongue inside. "I want you." He spanned her waist with needy hands and dragged her squarely on top of him to deepen the kiss.

She clutched at his shoulders, at his hair, at whatever she could reach—purring in her throat, breathing harder, faster, answering every foray of his lips and tongue.

"I want you," he whispered against her throat, nipped at her chin, kissed her again. With a powerful move, fueled by desire, he sat up with Beth on his chest and spilled her into his lap, swinging one foot to the floor and veeing his legs apart to relish the full impact of her fiery softness pressing against his hard arousal.

He peeled her shirt off over her head and pulled one of those peach-colored aureoles into his mouth to suckle on her even before her hands were free of the sleeves. She cried out his name on a startled gasp and raked her fingers into his hair, holding him against her while he squeezed the generous globe in his hand and feasted on the pebble-hard tip.

He kissed his way from one swell to the other, warming a damp path across her cool skin. "I want you." He fanned the words across her skin.

She moaned. He caught her twisting hips in his hands and held her still while he writhed helplessly against her.

Her busy hands wandered at will across his body. Scraping a palm across his grizzled cheek, sliding across his shoulders, trailing her fingers farther down as he shifted his attention back to her swollen lips.

"Kevin…" She went up on her knees to help him pull off her flannel pants. "Soon…"

Her fingers found his belt buckle, unsnapped his jeans, gently unzipped. "Don't make me wait."

He was shifting, moving, helping her in whatever way he could, speeding faster and faster toward his inevitable release. When her fingertips slid beneath the elastic of his boxer briefs, he lurched into her palm and then swore.

"Damn it." He snatched her wrist and pulled her back. He wasn't such a rutting bull that he'd let it happen this way between them. He wouldn't endanger her like that. "Stop."

"Kev?"

"Lady, you are the most beautiful thing I ever…" He sucked in a painful breath, framing her stunned face between his hands and begging her to understand. "I don't have a freaking condom with me."

Shock turned to disappointment in one hard, deep breath. But by the next breath, she was smiling. "*I* do." She pushed against his chest, trying to clamber to her feet. "If I can find them. I've never used them. Gag gift from my brothers when I moved. Protect myself from those big bad city boys, they said."

"Like me?"

For a moment she stilled. "Do I need protecting from you?"

Kevin shook his head, speaking straight from his heart. "You'll always be safe with me."

Beth leaned forward, planting a firm kiss on his mouth that promised she'd be right back. "I believe you."

Then she was up and stumbling on wobbly legs toward the hallway. "They're in the bathroom."

He didn't wait for her to return with the prize. He chased her down the hall, laughing with her as they opened three drawers in the vanity before finding a box of foil wrappers stuffed in the back. He lifted her onto the counter beside the sink and moved between her legs, shoving his pants down to his ankles and stepping out of them as her fingers fumbled with his to cover him. Wise or not, this woman ignited something in him that could no longer be delayed or denied.

"I can't wait." He pulled her to the edge of the vanity.

She wrapped her arms around his neck, wrapped her legs around his waist, giving herself to him in the most humbling way imaginable. "I don't want you to."

Kevin took her right there in the bathroom, sliding inside her welcoming heat. She buried her face against his neck as he held her tight and exploded inside her.

Once the tremors of her release subsided and her skin began to cool beneath his hands, Kevin backed away. He pulled a towel from the rack and gently tended their bodies. And before her toes could reach the floor, he scooped her up into his arms and carried her the rest of the way to her bedroom where he tucked her beneath the covers and crawled in behind her.

Beth must have dozed for a few minutes because the icy glow of the sunrise was reflecting off the snow outside her window and filtering into her bedroom when she next opened her eyes. She smiled serenely and settled against the furnace of heat warming her back.

Kevin's deep growly voice whispered against her ear. "Told you I was short on finesse. Have I scared you away yet?"

"No." She was feeling a lot of emotions right now—too many to sort out, perhaps—

but fear of Kevin Grove and the passion they'd shared wasn't one of them. "That was…exciting."

"I hope it's okay that I stayed."

"Of course." She squeezed the hand that rested on her hip.

"I wanted to wait around long enough to make sure you were okay."

She rolled over to face him, hating that he could still doubt that a woman could truly care about him—that *she* cared. She reached up to brush her fingertips across his stubbled jaw. "I think I'd be insulted if you were too eager to get away from me after…that."

"You were perfect."

"I wouldn't say—"

He silenced her with a quick kiss and lingered close so she could see past the hard jaw and crooked nose, and read the honesty in his warm, smiling eyes. "You'll get no complaints from me."

"Me, neither." This morning's encounter had certainly been nothing like her previous experience from college days. Kevin was a mature, virile man—not a boy in any sense of the word. And though her body ached from the sheer intensity of it all, she felt wickedly female and completely satisfied.

For one crazy hour, all the troubles in Beth's life disappeared across the snowy landscape outside her window. She was cocooned in the haven of her own home, her own bed, her lover's arms. This morning, there was only Kevin, only the weight of his body sliding over hers, only the keening pleasure of knowing that being with him made clear, perfect sense.

Later, he gathered her to his chest, pulled the covers over them both, and they slept.

"WHAT THE HELL is that?"

Not exactly the romantic good-morning greeting Beth had been dreaming about.

Once the startle of Kevin's curse zapped its way through her system, Beth was awake enough to realize the covers had been jerked down to her waist and he was sitting up on the side of the bed, staring at her bedside table. By the time the first shiver at the rude exposure to the house's morning chill registered, the weird electronic feedback from her alarm clock music was grating against her ears, as well.

"Sorry." Facing a wall of broad male back, she pulled the covers up to her chest and climbed onto her knees to reach around him and turn off the music. "It's been playing those annoying overtones for a while now. I'm guessing something's broken, or it's just getting worn—Kevin!"

He grabbed her wrist and stopped her from reaching past him. "How long has it been doing that?"

She looked down at the immovable hand, then up at his dark face, which was in dire need of a shave and a smile. If a bolt of lightning struck the air around them right now, she'd be back in that sci-fi nightmare of their first meeting on his front porch.

"I didn't realize it was that late." Feeling a need to appease this sudden stranger in her bed—and despising that he could bring fear back into her life just as surely as he'd erased it—Beth twisted her arm from his unresisting grip and scrambled off the bed. She pulled the afghan from the foot of the bed around her and backed toward the open door. "I'd better get my butt in gear or I'll be late for work. I'm going to hit the shower, okay?"

With little more than a nod of acknowl-

edgment to her, Kevin turned off the disso-
nant sound himself and then pulled the music
player from its port.

Yeah, it was good for me, too, you big goof,
she wanted to throw at him. But she kept her
smart mouth closed and shuffled down the
hall toward the bathroom. Whatever Kevin's
problem was this morning, she hoped it had
nothing to do with her. Still, a little tenderness would have gone a long way toward
assuring her that sleeping with him hadn't
been a freaky, one-time deal. She'd thrown
herself at a man who'd made it clear he didn't
want to get involved with a woman—that he
didn't trust relationships.

Daisy was in the hallway to greet her with
a lick of Beth's hand, and a rub against her
legs that knocked Beth aside a step. "Are you
trying to tell me something about your guy?"
she asked the dog. With a rueful smile, Beth
led Daisy to the French doors and put her out
in the back yard. "Go easy on him, hmm?"

Maybe tenderness the morning after just
wasn't Kevin's way. Maybe he'd already
given her all he had left in him to give.

Several minutes later, after Beth had
straightened the bathroom vanity to eradicate

the evidence of what they'd done in there last night, she blew her hair and stitches dry, wrapped a towel around her from chest to thigh and stepped into the hallway. She could hear Kevin on his cell phone out in the living room.

"…to sweep the house, Atticus. I can't tell you why yet, but I'm beginning to have an idea. No. I'll take care of it."

So, he was back in cop mode. The man she was falling in love with—her anchor through all this madness—was turning into a real Jekyll and Hyde. She'd gone looking for a protector that night she was attacked. She should be happy he was still willing to play that role for her. But it left her feeling a little melancholy to think that something which could have been pretty amazing between them was already slipping through her fingers.

"I'll call you back." She knew the moment he'd spotted her, padding down the hallway to her bedroom. "Beth, wait."

Keep it casual. Don't pressure the guy. "I'm running late. I expect you need to get to work, too."

His arm snaked around her waist from

behind and he hauled her up against the wall, pinning her there with his body.

Of all the… She swatted his chest in frustration. "Grabbing? Scaring? Hello—?"

When he covered her mouth with his hand to silence her, she was well and truly frightened. He wasn't pinning her after all. He was shielding her. From what?

Beth was marginally aware that he'd put on his jeans again and had holstered his gun at his belt. She was more aware of the press of rough denim against her thighs as her suddenly skimpy towel rode up her body. But she was completely aware of the dark warning written in his eyes, right next to the apology stamped on his fearsome features.

She nodded, understanding the request to keep quiet, and he slowly freed her mouth, brushing a wisp of hair off her cheek as he removed his hand. Her eyes tilted up and locked onto his, begging for an explanation.

"Get some clothes and whatever you need for a couple of days." His deep voice was barely a vibration against her ears. "You're coming over to my house."

"What?" She mouthed the question.

He settled his hands in a gentler position

at her shoulders and rubbed up and down the length of her arms, soothing her, apologizing. "I'm falling down on the job, lady."

She shook her head, denying it. But he stepped to the side and peered for a quick moment into her office before quietly shutting the door. Then his hand was on her cheek again. "There's a hidden camera in there," he whispered. "That's why the power light on your computer won't go off. It's running. There's a listening device in your bedroom—that's what was causing the feedback. I suspect your whole house is wired to watch you. Probably what that sicko was doing in here the night of your attack—setting it all up. I should have discovered it. I didn't even think to look."

"But I…we just…" She pointed to her bedroom and felt the heat leave her body. Humiliated—violated—afraid, Beth hugged her arms around her and leaned into Kevin's chest.

"I know." He hugged her tight for a moment, then kissed her hair and pushed her away. "That's why you're coming with me." He hunched his shoulders to look her straight in the eye. "I don't know how long they've been watching you—or what they hope to find. But it stops now."

"THEY'RE ONTO US." The big man had foolishly driven out to his house that morning instead of waiting for a more secure after-hours meeting in the board room.

Somewhere along the line, their simple plan had gone very, very wrong. Now he'd been forced to bring him into the security room on his estate where a wall of television monitors gave him access to key areas of his home, lab and office building—and other points of interest—like a plain beige ranch house in the suburbs of Kansas City. "I told you to get inside that house and remove every trace of your first visit there."

"I couldn't just strong-arm my way in—that cop was there. Grove is major case squad at KCPD. If you've been monitoring the mics and cameras, then you'd know that."

"Maybe he's just the boyfriend." Even though the house had been dark, there'd been no mistaking the sounds of healthy entertainment that had gone on in the wee hours of the morning. He'd been looking for more evidence that Elisabeth Rogers had been trying to open files on an encrypted GlennCo disk. And while his gut told him that disk contained a copy of the incriminating research data, after replaying hours of surveillance recordings, his own eyes had told him she hadn't been the one to type the blackmail letters. "Grove's interest in Miss Rogers could be purely personal."

"You don't believe that."

"No. I don't. Grove and Kincaid are the detectives working the body dumps you made on our failed research patients. Maybe he's using Miss Rogers to get to us. After all, Charles was using her to get the information out of the building." He picked up the remote and scrolled from one monitor to the next, trying to pick up any sign of what Elisabeth and Grove were up to next. But the house had gone quiet. Even the noisy dog was gone.

"Hey." The big man deigned to touch him. "I'm not willing to kill myself the way Landon did to get out of this mess. I've already got the blood of two men on my hands. You tell me how to fix this."

He pulled his sleeve from the big man's grip and tried to think of the best course of action. They still had a blackmailer out there whose identity continued to elude him. A blackmailer who'd be gravely disappointed if he found out a second copy of the research which proved Gehirn 330 had killed two of the patients it had initially helped was out there in the hands of a lowly secretary who was boinking a cop.

But Raymond Glenn couldn't afford to have anyone make public the results of the company's failed research. His fortune and position as CEO depended on it.

What if he stopped looking for a black-mailer, and let the blackmailer turn his focus on the competition—Elisabeth Rogers? Let one problem flush out the other. And if he kept a close enough eye on Elisabeth, then he'd be there when the blackmailer showed his hand. And he could kill two birds with one stone.

Kill being the operative word.

"Well?" the big man prompted.

He'd made tough executive decisions before. It was time to make one now.

Raymond looked at Tyler James and issued an order. "I want you to accompany me to the bank and then make a drop-off for me. I'm going to be cashing a one-million-dollar check as the first installment of payment to our friend."

"You're kidding me. You're giving in to that bastard's demands?"

He held up a hand to silence his man. "And then I'm going to enclose a courtesy note with the cash—alerting our blackmailing friend that he has competition for ownership of our secret."

Tyler smiled. He was getting it now. "And you might happen to let Elisabeth Rogers's name slip into that note?"

He nodded. "Don't approach her until the time is right. I don't want to tip our hand. But do not let that woman out of your sight."

"Yes, sir."

They'd eliminate them both. The cop, too, if he got in their way.

Chapter Nine

Beth had tried every argument she knew to convince Kevin to let her go in to work today so that she could run the flash drive on the GlennCo computers again to see if she could get a more useful grasp on the information it contained. Information she was certain Charles had wanted her to uncover—while someone else did not.

The offices would be short-staffed.

No.

She knew Dr. Landon's files and schedule better than anyone and would be able to find anything the police might need in their investigation into his death.

No.

There'd be people around the building, including security guards, and wasn't that the best deterrent to anyone who might want to follow her, spy on her, harm her again?

Kevin shrugged into his navy tweed jacket and turned to the mirror over his dresser. "You said they'd be short-staffed," he countered. "Not much of a deterrent in a building as large as GlennCo's."

Beth pulled a sweater from the moving box it had been jammed into, shook it out and proceeded to fold it into a loose square, smoothing out the wrinkles as she spoke. "Well, a few people is better than no one, right?"

He picked up the tie he'd laid out on the dresser and looped it around his neck. She shouldn't be enjoying the process of watching him groom himself and dress, transforming from big, bad monster man into big, bad cop so much. She was good and frustrated with him for asking her to remain a virtual prisoner in his home unless he or someone he trusted could be with her.

"What if I go to the police station with you?" she suggested.

His hands stilled at his collar and his gaze turned inward for one gloomy moment before he snapped back to the room and her and not letting her leave the house. "I don't think that's a good idea."

"Because of Sheila? Will your friends judge you because you're mixing police business with a…" What exactly was she to Kevin? "…a friend? Will they think you're using me just to solve a case?"

"My friends won't," he answered, indicating there might be others at KCPD who would question Kevin's motives for helping her. Or her motives for getting close to him. But neither was the excuse he gave her for staying away from the precinct offices today. "I've got some gruesome business to attend to this morning—talking to the M.E. from the crime lab. You don't want to be there for that."

Daisy snored, belly-up, on the dog pillow at the foot of Kevin's bed. One last argument to try. "Are you sure I'll be safe here? She's clearly not a guard dog."

"She sounds like one. Keep the doors locked and don't let anyone in—she'll scare 'em off."

"She about scared me off that first night. Who knew she just wanted to say hi and find out if I'd brought her a treat."

His big hands made surprisingly quick

work of knotting the tie. "If it makes you feel safer, I asked Hank to watch the house. And I've already called Alex Taylor—that young officer who patrols the neighborhood—to swing by a few extra times and keep an eye out for anything suspicious. He'll be here in two minutes if you need anything. I'll be here in twenty."

Fine. So the only thing that could really scare her today were the demons that could haunt her from her own mind.

Beth set the sweater on the bed and reached into the packing box for another. "Then what am I supposed to do all day? I don't want to go back to my own house until the crime scene team finishes sweeping for bugs. And even then, I don't know that I can ever shake the idea that someone's still there, watching me."

His gaze locked onto hers in the mirror. "I won't let that happen."

She wanted to believe him. But, "I don't feel safe when I'm alone anymore. I know I sound like a coward…"

"No." He turned and covered her fingers around the collar of the sweater, squeezing to stop their frenetic movement. "That sounds smart. You sound like a survivor."

She turned her hands into the security of his solid grasp and summoned a wry smile. "I wish I felt like one."

"Tell you what." He released her to slide his holster and gun into place on his belt, cinch it snug around his waist and then tuck his badge into his chest pocket, making the transformation into one of Kansas City's finest complete. "Can you keep yourself occupied for half a day?"

She'd seen the under-reconstruction bathroom before he'd gone in to shower and shave. "Do you have cleaning supplies?"

"I didn't bring you over here to fix up my—"

"Yes, I can keep myself occupied." Half a day of frustration being alone with Daisy the giant, snoring wonder beast, might be the best bargain she could make.

"Good. Then I'll be back at lunch and I'll take you to meet someone."

"Who?"

His craggy features curved with a grin. "Dig a little deeper in that box."

The rare smile was contagious. "I didn't think you played games."

"Just dig."

Beth quickly emptied the box until she found a small picture frame at the bottom. After she gently unwrapped the paper around it, she discovered a photograph of a petite woman with short, snow-white hair and a bright, mischievous smile. Although she barely reached his chest, the older woman stood proudly beside a somber Kevin in his dress blue KCPD uniform. "Is this your grandmother?"

"Miriam Grove." He plucked the silver frame from her hands and set it with great reverence on his dresser. "You'd be doing me a favor if you could entertain her for the afternoon. Make me feel a little less guilty about leaving either one of you alone so much."

How could she resist Miriam's smile? How could she resist meeting the one person who might be able to tell her about the real Kevin Grove? How could she pass up the opportunity to ask if her neighbor in battered armor had once been a prince before false charges and heartbreak had hardened him into the complex, cynical man he'd become?

Beth wanted to ask if there was any chance of finding that prince inside him again.

"Deal," she agreed. "Don't worry about me. I'll stay put until lunch."

Beth stood at the front window, peeking through a hole in the blanket covering it, watching until Kevin's SUV disappeared around the corner at the end of the block. She scratched behind the ears of the dog leaning against her thigh, finding what comfort she could in Daisy's acceptance of her as a friend.

But there was no real comfort to be had when the man who'd given her a job and trusted her with something more dear than his own life was dead. There was no comfort in knowing someone had broken into her home so he could watch her every move, hear her every word 24/7, without her even realizing it. Was she such an idiot that she hadn't known someone was spying on her? Was she such a little speck of unimportance in the world that a stranger thought he had the right to take that kind of advantage of her?

Shivering with a sudden chill, Beth leaned back a little against Daisy's muscular strength and glanced down the street in the opposite direction. Her Jeep was still parked in her driveway. Hank's truck was parked in front of his house. There was the Dixons' car, the Logans'. In fact, there were any number of vehicles sitting in driveways, warming up, or parked along the street that she recognized.

Or did she? Had she seen that truck parked in front of the Lentz home before? Was that red car new to the neighborhood? Was that Brenda Campbell all bundled up, scraping the ice off her windshield? Was there a man sitting in that car? A face at the window across the street?

Watching. They were all watching.

"Stop it!"

Daisy woofed as Beth jerked back from the window and the unknown terrors spying on her every move.

"I'm okay, girl."

But she wasn't. Her pulse was racing. Her breath came in erratic gasps and she was afraid. Stupidly, idiotically afraid.

Get busy. Do something. Stop thinking.

Would it be a total invasion of Kevin's privacy if she ran upstairs and put on one of those sweaters she'd folded? It wasn't just the warmth she craved, but the scent and security of the man who wore them that she wanted to surround herself with.

No. She could do this. She could take care of herself for a few hours before he returned. She was perfectly safe.

Disgusted at the paranoia her own imagination could frighten her with, Beth crossed to the first packing box she came to and started unloading books, counting the minutes until lunch.

And Kevin.

KEVIN PACED THE LENGTH of the table in the Fourth Precinct's interview room #3 as he listened to the speaker phone with Atticus. Dr. Holly Masterson-Kincaid, the chief M.E. for the KCPD crime lab, was giving her autopsy report on the two John Does whose mutilated bodies had been dumped in the warehouse district by the river.

Kevin was having a surprisingly hard time concentrating on the lists of details he normally catalogued in his head when he was working a case. Instead, his mind kept slipping in and out of the conversation, remembering other details.

Details like the way Beth Rogers liked to cling tight and purr against his skin when she was caught up in her emotions. Be it fear, anger, desire—she was a toucher. Her hands seemed to be in a perpetual state of motion—brushing, pressing, squeezing, stroking—right up until that moment when everything inside her seemed to fly apart.

And for a man who'd been tolerated, manipulated, even shunned by most of the important women in his life, her willingness—even eagerness—to touch and be touched by him was like some kind of magic spell. Beth Rogers made him feel whole again, made him feel hopeful.

Like all magic, though, the spell was destined to end. As long as she needed him as a protector and a cop, she seemed to be caught up in the same magic that flowed through his veins. But once this was wrapped up, once she found the answers she needed—and he would make sure she found them—once she felt safe, and returned to the day-to-day routine of the real world, whatever she was getting out of this relationship with him wouldn't be quite so thrilling or intriguing anymore.

And what he was getting—the chance to love and be loved like any other man on the planet—would be gone.

It was like Sheila all over again—charge to the rescue of a damsel in distress, get close, make love, introduce her to Miriam—lose everything. His heart, his pride, his willingness to trust. And although he was certain now that the danger surrounding Beth was as real as Sheila's had been manufactured, Kevin had little doubt the end result was going to be the same.

Beth would soon be gone from his life, and he'd be in a world of hurt.

Kevin reached the end of the table and picked up his coffee mug to polish off the tepid liquid. Yeah. Those were the kinds of details filling his head this morning.

"Detective Grove, did you get that?" A woman's voice was calling to him. "Kevin?"

Kevin's thoughts came back to the room, the call and the faxed photos spread out on the table in front of him. Dr. Masterson-Kincaid's report. "I'm here. Sorry, could you repeat that last bit? I zoned off for a moment—haven't been getting much sleep lately."

"I wondered," Holly laughed. "You usually eat up whatever facts I uncover. It keeps me on my toes to avoid being stumped by one of your questions."

"It's all a team effort," he assured her, setting down his empty mug and opening his notebook.

By the time he pulled out a pen to jot some notes, he realized that Atticus had leaned back in his chair and was watching him—intently. His partner knew where Kevin's thoughts had been. At the very least, he suspected.

"Is your head in the game today?" Atticus asked.

Kevin nodded. He wasn't about to admit to anyone, not even his partner, that a woman was once again getting in the way of his ability to do his job. In the end, being a cop would be the only thing he had to give his life any meaning. He'd do well to remember that. He turned from those all-knowing eyes and spoke louder so the phone would pick up his voice. "Doc? Let's get on with that report."

"The blood work on both your elderly John Does shows trace levels of an unknown drug. I imagine we'd find higher concentrations in the liver, which was removed. Without a comparison sample, though, I can't tell you what it is."

Kevin wrote down some possible leads to

follow up on. "Were they killed to remove the organs?"

"They weren't harvested for resale, if that's what you're asking," Dr. Masterson-Kincaid explained. "That was my initial hypothesis, even though an eighty-year-old organ would be hard to implant. They'd be potentially easy victims to coerce into signing a donor card—the brain tissue sample on both showed evidence of dementia."

Kevin glanced across the table at Atticus. "I hear a 'but' coming."

Dr. Masterson didn't disappoint. "But both men were dead at least twenty-fours before the impromptu surgery. Your first vic even longer than that."

"The organs would be useless by then."

"Exactly. And that's why there was so little blood at the crime scenes." The M.E. offered some other possibilities. "Maybe it was a failed medical procedure? Some serious malpractice?"

"Someone's destroying evidence."

Atticus nodded in agreement. "That's great, doc. At least that gives us a motive."

"Oh, and Charles Landon from GlennCo Pharmaceuticals?"

Kevin zeroed in on the abrupt change in topic. "Can you confirm the suicide?"

"Not unless the old man was a contortionist. You were right to suggest murder, detective." *Beth* had been right to call it murder. "I found an injection site at the back of his neck. I checked his medical records. He *was* on a combination of medications that could cause an extreme drop in blood pressure and trigger a heart attack. But he didn't have enough pills in his stomach to create an overdose. Whatever stopped his heart was injected directly into his bloodstream."

After a few more exchanges, Kevin and Atticus ended the call and set about organizing their investigative strategy for the day.

"I say we split up," Atticus suggested, gathering the photos and printouts and stacking them according to John Doe 1 and 2, and Charles Landon. "See if we can ID our Alzheimer's vics by age, treatment and physical condition—and find out who knew what Landon was taking and who had access to those drugs."

Kevin scooped up the third stack of faxes. "I'll take Landon. Beth will have the inside

track on who would have the means and opportunity to give him that extra shot."

Atticus leaned across the table and put a
hand on Kevin's notebook, stopping him
from walking away. "All the more reason *I*
need to take the lead on Landon's murder. It's
personal for you."

"You're talking personal?" Kevin argued.
"You went after your father's killer."

"Indirectly. I had this big bulldog of a cop
who took the lead on the investigation and
kept pushing me and my brothers out of the
way when we got too close. We showed up
only at the end because you needed backup."
Was there a point he was making? "Probably
saved all our jobs."

"I can separate my job from my personal
life. Sheila taught me that."

Atticus pulled back, shaking his head. "I
couldn't separate them when the people who
killed my father came after Brooke."

"That was different. You were in love with
Brooke. You married her."

But Atticus's cool-headed logic couldn't
be beaten. "And where were you when you
called me this morning?"

Kevin went still. Was he in love with Beth?

Yeah, he had the crazy hots for her. Any man with a conscience couldn't help but be concerned for her safety. But he couldn't be that big a fool to set himself up like that again, could he? Or had he already made that same mistake?

"I'm not marrying Beth." There'd be nothing between them once the magic ended. Permanence and happiness in Kevin's life, except for Miriam, were mutually exclusive.

"I'm not offering advice on your love life, pal. I'm just watching your back. You can't help Beth if you can't stay objective." It was a friendly caution to not jeopardize any case or career—or the woman trapped in the middle of it. "Can you?"

"Son of a bitch." He was right. Atticus Kincaid was always right. Kevin swiped the other stack of faxes from Holly and stuffed them into his notebook. "I'll take the John Does."

"YOU DID NOT SNEAK HER a cup of coffee," Kevin accused, not knowing which woman's smile was the prettier. Or which cat-that-swallowed-the-canary expression he should be more wary of.

"Relax, big guy," said Beth, scooting aside a tray laid with a coffee service on the table between the Oak Park solarium's matching love seats. "It's decaf. And I checked with the nurse first. She said an occasional cup wouldn't hurt her."

Kevin's day had been long and frustrating, conducting interviews on the phone and in person. Every fact he turned up on the two John Does had only led to more questions. The two upstanding victims had no fingerprint records in IAFIS—Integrated Automated Fingerprint Identification System—no missing-person reports which matched up. Identifying the vics through dental records was taking the lab extra time as neither man appeared to have visited any dentists in the Kansas City area. He'd made zip, zero, zed progress on his investigation today. Not a good day for a major case detective. It put him in a mood.

But that mood rapidly dissipated as he took in Miriam's animated expression from her perch on the flowered love seat. The sun was setting outside the bank of windows, casting a rosy glow across her angular features. She winked across the coffee table to the freckle-faced brunette sitting opposite her.

"I like Beth." Miriam lifted her near-empty cup with two hands to toast her new friend. "She doesn't put up with any guff from you."

Beth raised her cup in return. "We've had afternoon tea. Well, coffee—"

"And cookies."

"And calcium caramels. Which, by the way, are good for both of us."

"And are much easier to get down than those horse pills Yolanda used to try to give me."

Kevin dropped his notebook onto the coffee table and took off his gloves and coat. "Why do I think this wasn't such a good idea?"

Beth set her cup and saucer on the tray. "Well, this afternoon was much more enjoyable than cleaning the johns and unpacking all those books at your house this morning."

"You unpacked—?"

"You made your guest work?" Miriam scolded him.

"I volunteered." Beth defended him with a smile that didn't last. "At least here I haven't been looking over my shoulder all the time, jumping at every noise I hear. No hidden cameras. No time to think and worry about things I can't control."

Miriam nodded. "We've talked a lot about losing dear friends."

"You told her about Dr. Landon?" Not the murder part, he hoped. Kevin draped his coat over the back of the love seat and carefully sat next to Miriam.

"Oh, honey, don't sit here." She waved him across the way. "Sit over there with your girl so I can see you both."

"She's not my girl."

"Why not?"

That might be why putting these two together wasn't a great idea. Five hours in each other's company and they were thick as thieves. And judging by the approval in Miriam's smile, he could guess what the main topic of conversation had been between them. Him.

He reluctantly got up and moved to the seat beside Beth, hoping his grandmother's obvious matchmaking wasn't making her too uncomfortable. But it wasn't embarrassment he read on her face when she tugged on the sleeve of his jacket. She talked a good game in front of his grandmother, but fear and uncertainty still shadowed the depths of her eyes. "Did you find out anything more about Charles?"

He covered her hand where it rested on his arm, wishing he could drive those shadows away for her. "You were right. No way it was suicide. Atticus is following up on it. He might have some questions for you later."

"He's a good detective, right?"

"The best."

"Oh, did you find me a memento of Mr. Harrison?"

"What?" Kevin turned to find Miriam reaching for a photo sticking out from the corner of his notebook. "Grandma, no!"

He didn't know if it was his sudden jump or the graphic picture itself that made her gasp and clutch at her heart. Her cup clattered to the floor as Kevin quickly stuffed the crime-scene photo back into the binder and zipped it shut. But the damage had already been done.

She'd gone pale. Her breath came in quick, shallow gasps and tears had already clouded her eyes.

"Miriam?" Beth knelt on the floor beside

her, dabbing up the mess and laying a comforting hand on Miriam's knee.

Kevin sat beside her, letting her frail hand grab onto his, gently brushing the short, white curls off her face. "Do I need to call a nurse?"

But Miriam's eyes were still fixed on that notebook, her expression growing grimmer by the second. She squeezed her fingers around his thumb, silently communicating with him.

Well, hell. Kevin picked up the binder and pulled out the photo again. He did *not* want to ask this question. "Grandma…" He slowly turned the face of the dead man toward her. "Is *this* Mr. Harrison?"

Her body might be failing her, but her mind was still razor sharp. Miriam pushed the picture away. "Yes."

"I'm sorry." Kevin bent to kiss the top of her head. "I'm sorry."

"I'm all right, son." She caught his cheek before he stood, gently patting his face. "Do your job. Do it well." The tears spilled over as she pulled away. "Poor Mr. Harrison."

Kevin picked up his book, relieved to see Miriam calming. "Beth, do you have any photos of the people you work with?"

"The staff directory. It's in my desk at the office." She kept one hand where Miriam could hold on to her while she set the fallen cup up on the tray. "What is it?"

"A connection I don't want to be making, I'm afraid." He backed toward the archway exit, heading for the front desk to talk to someone about patient records. He pointed from Beth to Miriam. "You'll stay with her?"

"Of course."

Kevin turned, hurried. Not such a bad day for a cop, after all. He was about to break three murder cases wide open.

But not a great day for a man wanting to protect the people he cared about most. Because if he could prove that these three murders were all tied together by something shady going on at GlennCo Pharmaceuticals, then he'd just made Beth Rogers target one for the people who wanted to keep that connection a secret.

Chapter Ten

"I'd be happier about this if we had a warrant."

"Why?" Beth held the ring of keys she carried up to the beam from Kevin's flashlight, sorting through them until she found the one to unlock her office door. "Dr. Landon's report on the Gehirn 330 clinical trials is now public record since it was presented at the board meeting." She handed him the binder they'd retrieved from the GlennCo conference room and tucked her purse beneath her arm, freeing up both hands to find the key she needed. "It's not the first time I've had to get into the building after hours, so we're not trespassing. It's my desk, my things. Even that flash drive is mine because Dr. Landon gave it to me. I'm willing to voluntarily share them all with KCPD. At least I'm willing to share them with you."

The badge around his neck glinted in the light as he shifted the beam to the lock to guide her hand. Kevin Grove *was* KCPD. Right down to his boxer briefs and the cute little dimple he had on his... Beth dropped her keys, but Kevin's hand was there to catch them before they hit the floor. "Easy, lady." He pushed the key ring into her hand and moved in right behind her, using his body to shield her from unseen eyes and the three nighttime security guards they'd been avoiding since entering through the parking garage twenty minutes earlier. "Just get us inside and then we can debate the legalities."

She inserted the key into the lock, turned it and then Kevin was opening the door and scooting her inside, closing and locking it again behind them.

Blocking the light switch with his body, he swung the flashlight around to the computer on her desk. "All right. Let me sweep for any listening devices and then you can get it booted up. Show me what you've got."

Beth dutifully waited in the center of the room while he turned on a scanning device and inspected both her office and Dr. Landon's. In a matter of minutes, he'd deactivated a bug on each of their phones. Beth shivered inside the parka she still wore. "And *you're* worried about legalities?" She rubbed her hands up and down her arms. "I wonder how long my life has been an open book to these people?"

Kevin dropped the listening devices into plastic bags and pocketed them as evidence. And then he was behind her again, taking the coat off her shoulders and hanging it on the back of her desk chair. His hands replaced hers, massaging the length of her arms as he leaned forward and whispered against her ear. "Are you sure you want to do this? I'll get you out of here right this minute if you're having second thoughts."

She reached up and squeezed his hand on her shoulder. "No. I want this to stop. I don't want to spend the rest of my life feeling like every word I say is being monitored, like every shadow holds eyes that are watching me."

Looking into the corners of the familiar spaces where she'd been working for months now, Beth could imagine masked men and monsters and crouching creatures. She spun around to face the man she'd mistakenly labeled a monster at their first meeting. Kevin wore his villainous facade on the outside, but lived by a code of honor that could not be shaken. One or more of the men and women she worked with at GlennCo— the same men and women she'd admired, respected and had tried to emulate—they had proven to be the people she truly needed to fear.

Beth fingered Kevin's badge where it hung against his chest before sliding her hands inside the front of his jacket and trying to absorb some of the abundant strength that lay underneath. "Can't we at least turn on the lights?"

Kevin caught her hands and pressed them flat against his chest. "That's not how sneaking in late at night works," he teased. "I don't want Tyler James and his people finding out we're here." He backed her up a few steps until her wool slacks brushed against the chair. He sat her down, swiveled the chair to face the computer and kissed the crown of her hair. "Now, I'm giving you ten minutes to find something that proves those clinical trial results have been altered—and that there's motive for a cover-up. Whether we find anything or not…ten minutes. And then we're booking it out of here and getting you someplace safe." He repeated the argument he'd given when she'd first suggested they take another look at the data on the flash drive. "We'll come up with some logical reason to obtain a warrant to access GlennCo's computers."

Now that they were inside the eerily silent high rise, Beth was less inclined to argue. She reached up to squeeze the hand that rested on her shoulder and nodded. "Ten minutes."

By nine minutes, she had the computer running and the flash drive loaded. By eight, she'd typed in *Elisabeth* and had the HE4210 file open. After pulling a small flashlight from her purse, she opened the presentation binder and thumbed through the pages looking for a similar code so she could begin comparing data. "Should I be looking for something in particular?"

Kevin looked over from the window where he'd been watching some sort of activity on a rooftop or the street below them. "Arthur Harrison's name would be a start. Any discrepancies between the published report and the original data."

At six minutes, Beth hit pay dirt. "Arthur Harrison. Age 80. Oak Park Retirement Care Center grouping. Alzheimer's diagnosis… dates…sciencey stuff…yada-yada-yada… responds well to Gehirn 330," she read aloud as she skimmed the paragraphs before and after the poor old gentleman's name. "Here." She marked the spot on the screen and thumbed through the binder's printed pages, searching for a matching entry. Bingo. She held her fingers on both spots, indicating where Kevin should follow along with her. "Liver toxins rising dramatically. Countermeasures ineffective. Recommend termination of treatment."

He read the corresponding paragraph in the binder. "There's no mention of any side effects beyond stomach cramps. That's what Miriam said he complained of that last morning she saw him."

"So they knew his liver was failing and they didn't stop giving him the drug?"

"And when he died, they cut out the liver and disposed of the body, and continued administering the drug to other test subjects."

"Poor man." For a moment, Beth understood that what she'd suffered these past few days could have been much, much worse. "We have to ID the other subjects in the clinical trial and warn them of the danger they're in. That must be what Dr. Landon wanted me to do with the data."

"Four minutes." Kevin tapped his watch and thumbed toward the door. "Warnings come later. This gives me enough of a picture to fit all the puzzle pieces into so we can start building a case. I want you out of here."

Beth wasn't going to argue. "Now we just have to figure out how many GlennCo officials knew about the cover-up."

He closed the binder, indicating she shut down the computer, as well. "*We* as in Atticus and me. I'm putting you in a safe house as soon as I can arrange it."

"But I thought you—"

"Atticus?" Kevin was on the phone to his partner when the elevator door at the end of the hallway dinged.

Beth held her breath.

The sound was faint but distinct.

The soft rumbling sound of the door sliding open and the silence that followed was even more sinister.

"I'll call you back." Kevin folded his

phone shut and tucked it into a pocket. In the same silent motion, he pulled back his jacket and drew his weapon. "Can you kill the light from the computer monitor?"

He turned off his flashlight while she quickly closed down the files and computer screen. C'mon, c'mon, c'mon. Why was it taking so long to shut down? "Do you think someone knows we're here?"

"Could just be the guard making his rounds. I'll go check it out."

Beth shot to her feet and latched onto his arm. "You're leaving me?"

"If it's nothing to worry about, he won't see me."

"What if it is something to worry about?"

"Then I'll deal with it." He pried her fingers from his sleeve. "Lock the door behind me. I'll knock when I get back so you can let me in."

Almost as soon as the door closed behind him, the computer shut down, plunging the room into darkness. The moon outside the window was hidden by cloud cover, the stars nonexistent. The shadows in her office loomed large and closed in as Beth turned the lock and pressed her back against the frame.

Beth closed her eyes to block the ghostly images her mind was conjuring around the room, and tried to focus her hearing on the noises out in the hall. Her thundering pulse in her ears made it difficult to pinpoint exact sounds. One set of footsteps paused. A door creaked open. Why couldn't she hear two sets of footsteps? Where was Kevin? Were those footsteps any more real than the man who'd followed her through the garage in Kansas City?

A murmur of sound closer by popped her eyes open. The shadows still surrounded her. The dim moon glow chilled the room. The murmur became a rustle. Beth held her breath and pressed her ear to the door to listen more closely. *Kevin?*

The rustle became a whisper of air across the nape of her neck.

A shiver of terror drained the blood from her head straight down to her toes.

In the room.

She spun around. A tall shadow separated itself from the darkness.

Not her imagination at all.

A hand went up in the air, the syringe it held silhouetted against the window.

Beth threw up her arms, blocking the attack.

The sharp point of the needle pierced the sleeve of Beth's sweater and pricked the skin of her forearm before she knocked it away into the darkness.

A high-pitched yelp of pain grated against her ears, but it wasn't her own.

Tall figure. Slender build. Bright red nails.

A moment of stunned surprise was a luxury Beth didn't have. When Deborah Landon charged Beth with her bare hands, she lowered her shoulder and rammed into the other woman's gut with as much strength as she possessed. The two women hit the edge of Beth's desk and went tumbling over the other side.

"Beth!" Someone pounded on the door.

The chair tipped. The computer, keyboard and monitor crashed onto the carpet in a mini avalanche.

Deborah shoved the chair at Beth. "I want whatever Charlie gave you!"

"Are you crazy?" She dodged the rolling projectile and kicked out at the other woman's knees. "I don't know what you're talking about!"

"Beth!" More pounding.

As Deborah toppled, Beth dived on top of her, driving her hip into the other woman's stomach, pinning her wrists to the floor, trying to remember all the wrestling tricks her brothers had taught her.

"I need that information." Deborah's long blond curls got stuck between her lips, forcing her to spit the strands from her mouth. They were both breathing hard. Their blood was pumping fast. "It belongs to me."

"You know about the falsified research?" Deborah's big blue eyes swam out of focus.

"Where is it?" Deborah demanded. Beth's grip on her opponent was slipping. "I know Charlie gave you a copy. I told him we could both benefit from my plan. He could retire and we could go somewhere exotic together and we'd never have to worry about money again. But he wanted to tell the other board members. The stupid man."

"Don't call him…stupid." Beth's world tilted. Had she really just uttered such an inane thing? "He was trying to do…the right thing. And you…killed…him." What was wrong with her? "What did you do to me?"

The injection. Something had gotten into her system. She was feeling so weak.

"Beth!"

"Move out of the way!"

"No! Don't!"

She heard a loud crack of thunder. So unusual for this time of year. Two massive storm clouds blew into the room.

Not clouds. Men. *Focus.*

Not thunder. A gunshot.

Kevin threw Tyler James up against the shattered door and stripped the gun from his hand. "You son of a bitch—you could have hit one of them! Beth?"

Deborah turned her head to the side, smiled.

The flash drive. Knocked loose from the computer. Lying beneath the desk next to the partially empty syringe.

"Get off me!"

If Beth's reflexes weren't moving like slow-melting ice, she might have dodged the pain of Deborah's fist smacking against the side of her head. One of the stitches split and pain knifed through her skull.

If Deborah had been a little less greedy, she might have seen that Tyler James hadn't come to rescue her.

The moment Kevin turned to lift Beth in

his arms and carry her away from the struggle, Tyler scooped up the syringe and plunged it deep into Deborah's neck.

"We're not paying you another dime, you bitch."

The blonde was dead before Beth could scream.

Chapter Eleven

"I'm beat, Kev. How about you?"

Atticus pushed his chair away from his desk and leaned back to stretch out his long limbs as A. J. Rodriguez and Josh Taylor were escorting Raymond Glenn and Geneva Landon to their respective holding cells.

"We've got everyone's statements—including your eyewitness testimony regarding Deborah Landon's death. All the GlennCo board members involved in the cover-up are under arrest and the company is temporarily closed pending investigations by any number of government groups. And we've got legal aid sorting through that omnibus of research data to make sure any patients who were exposed to Gehirn 330 during the clinical trials understand what the lethal side effects might be so that they can speak to their own physicians. I also found out that *Gehirn* is the German word for *brain*." He closed the thick folder sitting on top of his desk. "And on that random bit of info, I'm going home to my wife."

Kevin was too exhausted to even laugh. It had been a long night, a long day, and if he gave it another twelve minutes, he could make it a long thirty-six hours that he'd been running on coffee and a few catnaps at the hospital where he'd been waiting for news on Beth's recovery. By the time her family from central Missouri had arrived, the doctors had told him she was out of danger and resting comfortably. Deborah Landon had only been able to inject a minimal amount of potassium nitrate into Beth's system. And while her blood pressure had dropped to a dangerous level, she was young and healthy enough that her body would completely recover.

Deborah, unfortunately, had received such a high dosage that her heart had stopped beating almost immediately. Kind of poetic justice for a woman who'd used the same means to murder her husband when he'd threatened to expose her blackmailing scheme.

"Are you heading back to Truman Medical Center?" Atticus asked.

He shook his head. "Beth's family is with her now. I made sure she was okay before I left."

"I was thinking more along the lines of whether you were okay."

"I'm fine." He scraped his palm over the stubble of his jaw. "I'm not the one who was in the line of fire."

Atticus rose from his chair, picking up his jacket and shrugging into it. "Are you that thickheaded that you don't know, or that thick-skinned that you don't care? That woman was into you."

"That woman *needed* me," Kevin corrected, standing to gather his things, as well. "I'm not going to force myself on her. She's young, gorgeous, smart, mouthy—and I'm…" Well, hell. Was this guy his partner or his therapist? "I'm going home."

"Well, what do you know." Chief Mitch Taylor stopped by Kevin and Atticus's desks. He'd just started B shift off on their day with the morning briefing. One of his announcements had been that they'd ID'ed the two John Doe murder victims through the

GlennCo data on the memory stick Beth had surrendered as evidence—Arthur Harrison and Franco Deltino would now be returned back to their extended families or estates for a proper burial, thanks to KCPD. Chief Taylor was still smiling about having good news to share around the holidays. "I assigned you two murders and you boys went and solved four and broke a conspiracy case. Congratulations."

"Thank you, sir."

"Thank *you*."

He shook hands with them both before Atticus asked, "So I take it we're dismissed, sir?"

Chief Taylor nodded. "You're dismissed. Grove? I need to see you in my office. Before you leave."

"Sir?"

The smile faded as his barrel-size chest rose and fell with a weary sigh. "I've had a complaint filed against you. By one of the women involved in the investigation."

"You're kidding me."

"Atticus, I'll see you on the next A shift. Grove, you're with me."

As he followed the chief down the hallway

to his office, Kevin replayed every moment of the past several days in his head. The only person he'd been remotely coercive with was Tyler James. The GlennCo security chief had been more than happy to make a deal and spill his guts about the people he'd taken orders from once Kevin had made it clear to him that terrorizing an innocent young woman—assaulting her, spying on her, firing a gun into a room where she was already under attack—was a surefire way to guarantee Kevin's personal appearance and professional testimony at each and every hearing the man had between now and death.

Atticus had interviewed and processed Raymond Glenn and Geneva Landon. Deborah Landon was dead. The only other person in all this who might file a complaint would be…

"I'll leave you to it, Grove." Chief Taylor opened his office door but made no move to enter. "I've got a meeting with the commissioner. Lock up when you're done. Like I said…" He winked. "Good job."

Well, hell.

"Kev?"

"Beth?" Mink-colored hair. Freckled cheeks looking a little paler than usual.

Kevin dropped his coat where he stood and hurried across the room to guide her back to the chair where she'd been sitting.

"What are you doing here?" He brushed aside the wisp of hair that clung to her cheek, checked the fresh bandage at her temple, knelt down in front of her to make sure her eyes were a clear gray-blue. "You should be in bed. In the hospital."

She wore the long brown coat that he'd first met her in over a pair of jeans and a plain, off-white sweater. She pulled off her gloves and squeezed and smoothed the leather in her busy hands. "They released me this morning. You once said that if anything...bothered me, that I could call you."

A protective anger fired in his veins, burning through his fatigue. "What's wrong? Are Glenn's lawyers already hassling you? Did Tyler James make some kind of threat?"

Squeeze the gloves. "I think…"

"You think what?"

Smooth the gloves. "You look awful."

"I get that a lot. A few hours' sleep and I'll only look half as ugly as I do now."

Her peachy mouth curved with the most serene, most generous of smiles as she squeezed the gloves again. "Not ugly. Never ugly."

Kevin covered her hands with one of his, stilling the nervous movement in her lap. "You think *what?*"

She waited. He worried. Beth spoke.

"That you love me."

Kevin's heart lurched inside his chest.

Where were the bad guys she needed defending from? Where was the mystery she needed him to solve? The truth she needed him to find?

So he'd been found out. He wondered what had given him away? The rush of concern? The hungry look? The bedside vigil that had ended only when her mother and father had arrived to take his place?

Reality check.

"And that bothers you?" Kevin pulled his hand away, rolled to his feet, put the length of the office between them before he could turn and say, "I would never force you into something out of gratitude."

"I know you wouldn't." She rose from her

chair, left the gloves behind. "That's one of the reasons I love you, too."

"You don't have to say that—"

"No, I don't." She took one step toward him and then another. "What bothers me is that…when I said a man was following me and no one else saw him, you believed me." Her chin tipped up, her eyes locked onto his. And she kept walking. "When I thought I was losing my mind, you believed I was sane. Yet when I tell you I love you…? Miriam said you'd be a tough nut to crack."

Beth was right in front of him now, filling up his head with vanilla and spice and faraway ideas about happily-ever-afters. "You talked to Miriam?"

"She said to go for it. To 'man up' and tell you how I feel." Beth's mouth twisted into an adorable frown. "I don't think she quite grasps how that phrase works, but she told me she gave some similar advice to you."

Something inside his chest cracked, leaving him a little breathless. He threaded his fingers into the velvety softness of her bangs and brushed them away from her forehead to press a kiss there. Her eyes drifted shut and he dropped petal soft kisses on the tip of her nose, the edge of her bandage, the bow of her lips.

Emotion welled up inside him and eased out on a mix of a laugh and a sigh. "I don't think I can fight both you and Miriam. And I guess the chief's in on it, too. And Atticus."

She rested her hand over his heart as she blinked her eyes open. "In on what?"

"Believing."

The spell of distrust that had encased his heart crumbled into dust. With a whoop of joy, Kevin scooped Beth up in his arms, crushed her against his chest and claimed her mouth in a deep, possessive, wild kiss.

Her hands were around his neck, in his hair, inside his collar by the time he let her toes touch the floor again. "You totally grabbed me that time," she accused.

"You were grabbing back, lady."

"So you *do* love me?"

"Yeah."

"Yeah?"

"Yes."

Beth smiled. Kevin Grove never promised anything he didn't know for a fact. "I believe."

* * * * *

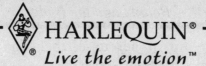

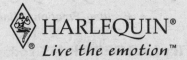

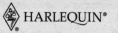

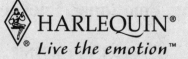

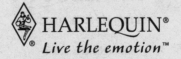

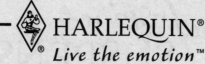

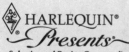

Love Inspired®
SUSPENSE

RIVETING INSPIRATIONAL ROMANCE

These contemporary tales
of intrigue and romance
feature Christian characters
facing challenges to their faith...
and their lives!

**Four new Love Inspired Suspense titles are
available every month wherever books are
sold, including most bookstores, supermarkets,
drug stores and discount stores.**

Steeple
Hill®

Visit:
www.steeplehillbooks.com